HESTER BIDGOOD

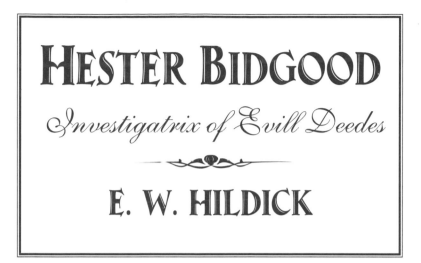

HESTER BIDGOOD

Investigatrix of Evill Deedes

E. W. HILDICK

Macmillan Publishing Company   New York

Maxwell Macmillan Canada   Toronto

Maxwell Macmillan International
New York   Oxford   Singapore   Sydney

First edition. Printed in the United States of America
10 9 8 7 6 5 4 3 2 1
The text of this book is set in 12 point Stempel Garamond.

Library of Congress Cataloging-in-Publication Data
Hildick, E. W. (Edmund Wallace), n.d.
Hester Bidgood, investigatrix of evill deedes / by E. W. Hildick. — 1st ed.
    p.   cm.   3-95 Jtic A4J /J.
Summary: Thirteen-year-old Hester Bidgood and her fifteen-year-old friend Rob Macgregor investigate the stoning and branding of a kitten in a New England town caught in the grip of witchcraft rumors during the year 1692.
ISBN 0-02-743966-6
[1. Cats—Fiction. 2. Witchcraft—Fiction. 3. New England—Fiction. 4. Mystery and detective stories.] I. Title.
PZ7.H5463Hg   1994
[Fic]—dc20   93-47919

Contents

HESTER BIDGOOD

1
The Jagged Cross

A black-and-white hog was rooting in the garbage scattered outside one of the meaner houses. The gaunt, ragged figure of a man stood stooped under the eaves of the meetinghouse, with his hat in his hand and one ear pressed against the wooden wall.

Except for them, the main street of Willow Bend was deserted at two-thirty in the afternoon on that last Thursday in March 1692.

There had been a heavy thunderstorm during the morning. Water gleamed in ruts the whole length of the street. Outside the meetinghouse and Cleary's tavern opposite, the puddles were fewer. There were large flat stones outside the meetinghouse and cobbles in front of the tavern. But there was still much mud, even here, oozing up into all the cracks and gaps.

That was why rushes and cattails had been strewn outside the meetinghouse before the start of the Reverend Phipps's Thursday lecture. And also why a load of dry gravel had been spread in a broad path between the house of worship and the tavern. Ezra Cleary had seen to that. The subject of the lecture promised to be of great, if dreadful, interest to the townsfolk, and it was expected that there'd be many who would wish to discuss it afterward over cakes and cider.

"See you bake plenty of tartlets and sugar buns," Cleary had told his wife, his eyes gleaming greedily from the folds of his cheeks. "Methinks trade will be brisk."

There had been another downpour during the lecture—short and with only a single thunderclap. Already the pale gray of the gravel was deepening to black, and there were still hailstones glistening between the ruts and on the rushes. Only on the paving stones had they melted away. For sure, there was what looked like a drift of these icy particles blown together on one of the stones.

But it was in fact a limp, sprawled bundle of fur: the body, seemingly lifeless, of a young cat.

Suddenly, the eavesdropping figure straightened up. The man put on his battered high-crowned hat. He looked quickly toward the street, then toward the graveyard in back of the meetinghouse, and made off in the latter direction. The piping tones of Mr. Phipps had been replaced by a rumble of voices rising and falling in prayer. The congregation was about to disperse.

Just at that moment, the mud-spattered hog seemed to notice the limp bundle. It had been steadily drawing closer and now it lifted its steaming snout, sniffing. But then the doors of the meetinghouse burst open, and people began to emerge—some with white, uneasy faces, others flushed. The hog grunted and moved off across the street and down an alley at the side of the tavern. This led to the jail, the pillory, and the scaffold. It was almost as if the hog sensed there might soon be rich pickings there.

No one noticed the cat at first. Many were making straight for the tavern and were halfway across the street when the cry went up.

"'Tis a dead cat!"

"Aye! Goody Willson's!"

"So it be! Her familiar!"

The word *familiar* arrested everyone. It had them squelching and scuffling back to where a small group was bending over a stone under the great sycamore between the meetinghouse and Mr. Phipps's manse.

Nobody reached down to move the animal's body to a less exposed place.

Already it seemed a dark omen. Had not the lecture been about witchcraft and the rumors that had lately been drifting down from the colony to the north? Rumors of arrests made in the Massachusetts village of Salem? Of the devil laying siege to the whole of New England?

Had not Mr. Phipps been laboring to calm their fears and to assure them that all would be well if they continued to pray for God's protection? Well, they *had* prayed.

And now *this*!

There was no mistaking whose cat it was. Even in those days the breed was beginning to die out: the old English plain gray, with two broad black bands on its forelegs and a black tip to its tail. This was the traditional grimalkin of the legends—a witch's cat every inch.

The appearance of the creature did seem truly threatening, lying there outside the meetinghouse. Lying where it had not been when they'd gone in. Lying in wait for them.

And with a new mark on its flank, the like of which they'd never seen before.

"What—what *is* it?"

"'Tis a cross, noddy! A jagged one, but a cross!"

"Hush! Here she comes. . . ."

2
Accusations

The crowd parted eagerly to make way for a bulky elderly woman. She had haunted, bewildered eyes. She'd been to the lecture and as usual was dressed neatly, but already she was in some disarray. Her cap had slipped and a silky iron gray braid had started to unravel. Her speech was normally indistinct because of the lower teeth, brown and ugly, that overlapped the few she had left at the top. But now she sounded fuzzier than ever as she croaked, "Grayling! . . . My love! . . . Wha-what—?" Then she screamed.

Bending to the cat, she had seen the mark.

Suddenly she lurched, looking around, her eyes terrified now, questioning, pleading. The jutting brown teeth began to move up and down rapidly, rhythmically. But no sound emerged, and all at once her eyes rolled upward, then closed.

The person nearest grabbed her. Young Hester Bidgood had been bewildered and horrified. But she had the presence of mind to realize that a sudden fainting fall might cause serious injury to a woman as heavy as Goody Willson.

Even so, she was too heavy to hold completely. Hester had to let her slump to the ground as gently as possible. With her arm around Goody Willson's shoulders, keeping her head raised, she took care to put her own body between the still-closed eyes and the creature's body.

"Come, Hester. Do not get involved."

Hester glanced up at her aunt and shook her head. She was a grave-looking girl for thirteen. She tended to hold her chin close to her chest, which made her look not only plumper than she really was but also touchy and even dull. But her clear green eyes had a spark in them now, matching the bright red curls that strayed from under *her* cap. Hester was getting angry.

"Won't someone please—?" she began.

"That is all right, my love. Let me take some of the weight."

"Thank you, Nell," said Hester to the portly middle-aged woman who had come to kneel at her side. The newcomer was already unfastening Goody Willson's cap strings.

The onlookers were finding their voices again.

"See how she shrank from the sight of the cross?"

"Aye—and then did swoon! 'Tis an act of God. A punishment."

"So it be!" rose a screech. "A punishment for her witching ways!"

Everyone turned to the speaker.

It was Peacemaker Cleary, also thirteen, the son of the

tavern keeper. He had pushed his way to the front. He was a scrawny, gangling youth, with dirty yellow hair straggling from under his hat. His manner was twitchy and squirmy, and while his eyes bulged with indignation, he still wore his usual lopsided grin. A bunch of younger children clustered around him, parroting his words.

"Witchy ways!"

"Witchy Willson!"

"Witchy Gammer Willson!"

Goody Willson stirred. Her eyes flickered open. "W-witching ways?" she murmured.

"Pay no heed to them, Mistress Willson," said Hester. She caught sight of another figure coming to the front. "Rob—do something about that poor creature, for heaven's sake!"

The newcomer was a couple of years older—and several inches taller—than Peacemaker Cleary. His movements were lithe, compact, catlike. He gently pushed aside one of the children and knelt down by the body.

Peacemaker Cleary was still looking at the animal's owner. "Ho, yes, Goody Willson!" he screeched. "I have seen 'ee! I have watched your shape at nightfall, flying acrosst the fields and into the trees! I have—"

"Hold your tongue, Peacemaker Cleary!" snapped Hester. "Can't you see she is distressed?"

Goody Willson had fallen into another swoon. Rob MacGregor, still kneeling over the cat, murmured something that sounded like, "Strange!" His eyes were puzzled. At first he seemed not to hear Peacemaker's renewed accusation as the boy pointed at Hester and said:

"Ho! And here be *another*! Here be an apprentice witch! Here be—" He broke off as something made him turn.

Rob was scowling at him fiercely. Peacemaker dried up at once, and some of the youngest children started backing away. They had been taking advantage of their unusually close-up view of the tall youth's face to see if it were really true that his nostrils and ears had been pierced to hold silver rings while he'd been living with the Indians.

Rob's face softened as he turned to Hester. "It breathes, Hester. Maybe it will live yet."

This seemed to prod Peacemaker out of his silence. "Hear that?" he cried. "Another! An Injun savage! A devil's imp! A witch's familiar hisself! Always with the witchy women! Injun savage! Son of a squaw! A—"

"Be silent, boy!"

The crowd parted again as the Reverend Phipps approached. He was a tall man with a scraggy neck. His cheeks were purplish. This sometimes gave him the look of an angry turkey, but his eyes were a mild blue.

"Rob MacGregor is as white as you or I," he said, staring at Peacemaker Cleary. He turned to Nell. "What is the trouble, Mistress—oh!"

He had seen the cat.

Still kneeling, Rob was cradling it carefully on his black woolen cap. Some of the smaller boys had edged up closer again to inspect at close range the rather ragged, tufted way his hair still seemed to sprout at the top of his head. Darker than Hester's, it was nevertheless easy to see why it had earned him the name Blazing Scalp among his former captors.

But Mr. Phipps was staring at the damage that had been done to the cat's hair, not Rob's.

"What in the world did *this*?" he murmured.

"A bolt of lightning?" suggested Magistrate Lawson, who had walked up with him.

Peacemaker now kept a respectful silence.

"Aye, sir," one of the adult bystanders said. "You can see where the fur has been singed. 'Tis the mark of God."

"Yea, the mark of God!"

Everyone turned to the latest speaker. A ripple went through the crowd. Some were nudging others. Some were openly grinning and tapping their foreheads. Trust Crazy Eben to have his say in a matter such as this!

The tall, gaunt eavesdropper was standing at the fringe of the crowd, his eyes glowing. It looked as if at one time, long ago, his hat had been used to put out a fire and the brim had been scorched and nibbled by flames. His white beard seemed streaked with soot even now. And the branded letter *H* on his left cheek was a raw, fiery red after being pressed against the meeting-house wall earlier.

"'Tis God's sign to remind ye that the end of the world be nigh!" he said. "This cat, this kit, is but one year old, no more. What would be its natural span but eight, nine years? And in eight, nine years, what then? 'Tis when the world will end, good people. In flames. In fiery, furious, sulfurous flames. On the last of December, sixteen hundred and ninety-nine!"

Mr. Phipps had turned away. He had heard all this before. Besides, as everyone knew, he always felt somewhat ashamed in the presence of this crazy old man, who had been treated so harshly as a heretic by one of Mr. Phipps's own predecessors.

"Is the woman recovering, child?" he asked Hester.

"She will, sir," she replied, "if she isn't so closely pressed."

"Of course," muttered the minister, turning to the crowd. "Stand back!"

This left Rob more exposed as he stood there nursing the cat.

"Take care that she doesn't see that again when she opens her eyes," Hester said softly but urgently.

Rob nodded. "I will remove it now."

"Yes," said Hester. "Do. The woodshed."

Rob slipped away. No one paid him much attention. All eyes were on Goody Willson again. She had started to groan and writhe convulsively. It now took Nell and Hester all their strength to hold her still.

And then the words came.

With lifted head and blind, tearful eyes, Goody Willson started bellowing out curses on whoever had done that to her poor kitling—curses so heartfelt and choking that they seemed to be forcing their way through feathers.

White-faced, Peacemaker Cleary found his tongue again. "Hear that?" he yelled, dancing up and down. "She curses the one who made the mark! She curses God hisself! They be *witch's* words!"

Even Mr. Phipps looked shocked.

And suddenly Goody Willson's body slumped and she fell silent, breathing heavily.

There was silence all around.

"Come," whispered Nell. "Let us take her home before things get too far out of hand."

3
The Captive's Return

"Rob! What are you *doing?*"

When Hester opened the woodshed door, she thought for a second he was about to cut the cat's throat.

The animal was laid out on a tray on top of the waist-high pile of pine logs that lined one side of the shed. Rob was holding a large pair of kitchen scissors. The points were pressed into the fur under the creature's chin. Maybe he had *already* done it, she thought, as she darted forward. The cat lay very still.

But there was no blood. Not at that spot, anyway.

Rob ignored her question. There was a deep line between his eyes. Then, with a snip of the scissors, he deftly pulled away a short length of twine.

"That must have been nearly choking her," he said, placing the twine on a sheet of paper at the side.

Hester felt a new pang—suddenly more hurt than shocked. The paper bore the scrap of verse she had so carefully printed out for him with her finest quill and best black ink, only a few weeks earlier.

However, she dismissed this from her mind when she

noticed that there were other things laid on the paper: three small greenish gray spiky burrs; a fragment of blue that looked like a petal; and a long white hair that showed up only where it crossed the black lines of verse.

"From the cat," he said. "In its fur."

She looked at the sprawled body. She could see no white markings at all.

"No. Not one of its own hairs," said Rob. "It is too coarse and crinkled. 'Tis that of a dog."

"But—"

The animal twitched. One eye had opened slightly. Rob stroked the fur just above it, very gently, with the tip of a finger. The eye closed and the animal's flank heaved with what might have started as a sigh but ended with a spasm. A faint mew broke from its lips.

Hester noted a spot farther back on its head where the fur was matted.

"She is in pain," Rob murmured. "She has had a blow on the head. The warmth from the lamp is thawing out the pain. I must bring medicine. I will not be long."

"But—"

"She will be all right until I return. She must lie there and be still. She knows that. Be sure *you* do not move her bones, thinking to soothe."

"Has she broken some?"

"I cannot tell for sure. Her rear left leg might be broke. Mayhap there be only bruises."

"Should I bathe this lightning burn?"

Rob shook his head. "No. Leave it to me. . . . And that was no lightning strike!" he added.

Hester stared at the singed and blackened fur. "You think not?" she whispered.

"No. I have seen many trees stricken by lightning, and once a man. It bit much deeper. And it never left a mark shaped like this."

"So what made *this* mark?"

"Not lightning. And not God. The Great Spirit would not need to tether the creature before making his mark. Now I must go."

"Tether?"

"I must go," he repeated.

"Your cap," she said.

"Leave it lie," said Rob. "She is used to its scent and warmth. It's her only comfort until I can apply the balms and poultices she needs."

Hester looked at the tray with its shallow basketwork sides. It was the one on which she took her aunt's meals and medicines when she was unwell in bed. Rob must have gone straight to the kitchen for the scissors and found the tray there.

"But if it tries to clamber out and follow—"

"She will not do that," he said. "If she does get restive, just stroke her gently—so." He put his finger lightly on the fur between the cat's eyes. "And murmur something soft."

"Murmur *what*?"

"Anything, so long as it sounds healing and renewing." Rob paused and grinned, pointing to the sheet of paper. "'Good King Robert's Testament.' . . . It helped save *my* life once!"

After Rob had closed the door behind him, she took

another look at the paper. At least he had kept it clean up until now, she thought. But she was not so pleased to note the creases' looking so sharp and undisturbed. She'd hoped he would have been continually opening it and studying it. She had been counting on it as the key to his further education. Now she was not so sure. . . .

Everything had gone so well at first, too, from the time twelve months ago when Rob had been ransomed and old Mr. MacGregor had begged her to help teach his grandson to read and catch up on those seven lost years.

There *had* been one awkward moment at the very beginning, of course. She smiled, even as she thought of it.

"Why you?" the youth had asked. They were his very first words to her.

He was still grim and scowling in those days, and not at all certain in his speech. Not at all pleased to have been taken from his Indian friends either.

"Why *me*?" she echoed, puzzled.

"Aye. Why you to teach me? Why you and not school?"

"Mr. Williams says he fears you will get angry when the young ones mock you."

His scowl became thunderous. "Mock *me*? Blazing Scalp? Why would they dare mock *me*?"

"Because . . . because you are older. A great older boy. Yet not able to spell your letters."

"Huh!" The thundercloud remained.

"So you *would* get angry, wouldn't you?"

"Much!" he said.

"And then you *might* hurt them?"

"No!"

She was surprised. He was still glaring angrily.

"No?"

"No," he growled. "I would *kill* them!"

"K-kill them?"

"Aye! And take their scalps and hang them on my belt!"

She gaped at him.

Then he laughed. Howled and stamped and shook with laughter, doubling up.

"What is so funny?" she demanded.

"Thy ... thy *face*! ... Oh, ha-ha-ha! You *believed* me!" He struggled to control his expression. "Think you that young *Indian* children don't jeer and scoff at the older ones? And think you the older ones scalp them just for *that*?"

"I—why? What *do* they do?"

"Scorn them!" he said haughtily. "Frown them into silence. Or—if they keep on—chase them."

"And then what?" she asked—frostily now.

"Why, tumble them to the ground. Or throw them in the river. Or into a thornbush. Or—oh, there are many places to throw them which they do not like. Into the horse dung was my choice. But scalp them—no. Ha-ha-ha!" So he began that revolting laughing again.

She could never abide being laughed at. Big and fierce as he was, she flashed back, "Very well! Enough! Or— or I will roll *thee* in the horse dung!"

Their friendship might have ended right then. For a few seconds, he looked offended. Then he burst out laughing again, and this time it was so free and infectious that she couldn't help joining in.

"Ho-ho!" he had gasped finally, tears running down his cheeks. "I like thee, Hester Bidgood! You may teach me my ABCs. I am ready."

Which is exactly what she did, over the next few months, mainly out-of-doors. They looked for the alphabet letters in the markings on flowers, leaves, bird and butterfly wings—even in the shapes of clouds. Then they traced them out with their fingers or sticks, in sand or mud, or painted them on their arms with red dye from bloodroot plants, or even soot from charred sticks.

After that they progressed to matching shapes of certain creatures or objects with their initial letters. Like *S* for *snake,* if one happened to be curled in that fashion. Or similarly *S* for *squirrel,* if its tail should be cocked like that. Rob himself suggested *A* for *arrowhead,* and the day he connected *T* with *tomahawk* and *P* with *pipe* was a red-letter one indeed.

But in the fall, things had begun to change. When it came to *reading* there'd been a great dropping off. Much of this had been due to the dull texts that she'd borrowed from Mr. Williams—the religious mottoes and proverbs that most children were forced to practice with.

Also, of course, there was the fact that during the colder months the lessons had to be conducted indoors—which he hated. Whether it was in this drafty woodshed or the snug warmth of the room that Mistress Brown had put at their disposal, he complained that he couldn't breathe freely.

Then, just as she was giving up hope, she'd hit on the idea of copying out something from his own memory, something he knew by root-of-heart, something that meant much to him. She hoped that by matching well-known words to printed signs, he would suddenly get the *feel* for reading.

She looked at those lines now, ignoring the piece of twine, the white hair, the petal, and the burrs.

> On foot should Scottishe warriours go,
> With hylls and bogges behind them,
> Let woods for walles be their defence
> Where enemys cannot find them.
>
> With wyles and wakings of the night
> And dreddeful noises made on height,
> Foes shall ye turn with mortal fear
> As chased with bow and sword and speere.
>
> This be the counsel and intent
> Of goode King Robert's testament.

And yes, she thought. Even if those lines hadn't actually saved his life, at least they'd made Rob's captivity much less of an ordeal.

She forgot about his learning difficulties and even the cat, as she tried once more to picture the scene in the smoky Indian lodge, with the firelight flickering on high cheekbones and glinting in dark, unblinking eyes, as the chiefs listened intently to those lines that came stumbling from the lips of the seven-year-old captive. . . .

4
The Investigators

A faint mew interrupted her thoughts.

Leaving the small, white captive to recite his crude lines to the chiefs of a band that had so recently killed his parents and brothers, Hester turned back to the present.

The cat's eye had opened again. Still only a crack. It seemed to be appealing to her for relief. She remembered Rob's words. She put out a finger and began gently stroking the creature between the eyes.

Then, feeling rather foolish, she started to recite those fierce warlike lines herself—but in a soft and soothing voice, as if it were all about lambs and babes and lullabies instead of weapons and warriors and sudden death.

> On foot should Scottishe warriours go,
> With hylls and bogges behind them,
> Let woods for walles—

"*Hester!* What—what—?"

Hester looked up, startled. Her aunt had come in very quietly.

"Whatever are you doing?" said Aunt Elizabeth. "That is Goody Willson's, is it not? It is! I can see it is! What is it doing here? *And on my tray!*"

The more her aunt fussed and panicked, the more Hester tried to remain calm. She felt sorry for this weak, ailing woman, who had been so kind to Hester since she'd been orphaned at the age of two.

"Well, child?"

"It is sick, Aunt."

"I can see that! Is it infected? Have you been *touching* it?"

"It isn't dying of the plague or smallpox, Aunt," said Hester, keeping her voice low. "If it *be* dying, it is of an injury. It has been almost murdered."

"Well!" said her aunt, letting her chin recoil in indignation. (Hester had to close her eyes for a moment. There were times when she dreaded that she herself might grow up to look like her aunt: short and dumpy, with pepper-and-salt hair and pasty, flabby cheeks.) "But it was stricken by *lightning*, child! *God* is not a common murderer. He hath his reasons."

"It was no lightning strike, Aunt," said Hester, echoing Rob's words. "It—"

Which was when Rob himself walked in. "Good evening, Mistress Bidgood," he said.

All at once Hester's aunt relaxed. She even managed a small smile. "Rob," she said. "I—I see you have brought medicine."

Rob nodded and unhitched the fringed bag from his shoulder. He gave the cat one quick glance, then turned back to the woman. "Aye, Mistress Bidgood. Salve for its wounds. Furniture for a poultice. A mild—"

"Yes, yes, but hast thou brought some of thy sweet-goldenrod root? My colic has suddenly griped me again."

Hester suppressed a groan. Aunt Elizabeth was always imagining she was starting some terrible disease. That was why Rob was a favorite of hers. Her opinion of his herbal teas and other healing brews couldn't have been higher.

"No, alas, Mistress Bidgood," Rob began. "I have only brought sufficient for—"

"Tsk!" went her aunt. "Humans should always come before mere animals, young man!"

"Oh, Aunt!" Hester protested. "We *have* some of that root already. I brought it from Mistress Brown's herb garden myself."

The woman sniffed. "I know, child. But it is not the same. Only Rob knows where the best herbs grow."

"Yes, Mistress Bidgood," said Rob. "And the first thing tomorrow I will bring you some fresh from a field corner I know."

That seemed to placate her some. "But—"

"In the meantime," he said, reaching into the bag—as patient with her as when he was tickling a trout or stalking a rabbit, Hester thought—"if you use the root Hester speaks of, and add this to the infusion, 'twill bring you *some* relief."

"Thank 'ee, thank 'ee, Rob!" the woman said, almost snatching the wrinkled leaf he handed her. Then: "See ye do not put your nose too near that creature, Hester!" she said, hurrying off.

"What *was* that leaf?" Hester asked when the door was closed.

Rob shrugged. "Just something for the cat's poultice." He smiled. "'Tis harmless enough." Then his smile vanished. "But now we must busy ourselves."

One of the things that sometimes annoyed Hester about her friend was the way he ordered her around when doing a job. Fetch this, fetch that, hold it out *so,* put thy finger here, hurry, not so fast, be careful. . . .

This time he did it more than ever. For the next half hour he had her running back and forth to the house, under the green clearing sky streaked with orange from the setting sun. Hot water, clean clouts, a mixing bowl, more hot water—his requests came crackling over his bent shoulders. Even her aunt was kept at it, refilling the kettle and cutting fresh strips of linen, protesting all the time, "But I will not have it in the *house!* Mark that! Not in *this* house!"

Hester hadn't minded Rob's briskness today. After all, he himself wasn't idle for a second, so busy was he snipping, binding, pasting, mixing, and softly—so softly—rubbing and prodding. Once, she'd come in with a steaming bowl to find him with his ear close to the cat's chest. She even caught him scraping dirt from between its claws on one occasion.

Finally, when she saw the cat lying there poulticed and splinted—with the wound on its head and the singed cross glistening with what must have been a soothing grease, judging from one deep sigh that heaved its flank—she smiled. It was her *great* smile, as Nell called it, adding that that was when she really did look pretty. The one she could never conjure up cold, no matter how hard she tried. It needed no coaxing now, though. "You have done well, Rob," she said.

"Hmm! *We* have done well," he said, still frowning at the cat. "Thus far."

Her smile faded.

"Why? Do you fear she will not mend?"

"Not if she stays here. She needs continuing warmth and encouragement. . . . I *could* take her to my grand-parents' house," he added. "But . . ." He gave her an inquiring glance.

She took a deep breath. The air in the shed was fragrant now with ginger and cedarwood, wintergreen and catmint, as well as pine pitch. Then she shook her head.

"I'm sorry, Rob. My aunt has made it very clear that she doesn't want the creature in our house. I think she really does believe it could be a witch's familiar." She gazed down at the cat and sighed. "How could anyone think that such a poor, innocent creature would be the devil's instrument?"

"Many seemed to believe it," he said. "Out there. This afternoon."

Suddenly, looking at the splints on its hind leg, she felt a flush of anger burn her cheeks. "Aye! And some more than others. *One,* anyway."

"Who?"

"The one who was the *real* doer of this deed! Not to speak of the even more terrible deed likely to follow it."

Rob still looked puzzled.

"Don't you *see?*" she said. "It isn't just the cat whose

life is—has been—in danger. If the people continue to believe it an act of God, they will believe Goody Willson is a witch. They—they might even hang her for it!"

"Ah!" he murmured, nodding.

"Yes—ah!" she said. "So, as I say, we must find out who was that real evildoer. And discover him to the people."

He frowned. "Yes, but—how?"

"By—" Suddenly Hester remembered a word she had lit upon while browsing in Mistress Brown's great dictionary. "By being *investigators*," she said. "By using the signs to track that evil person down. The way you use footprints in the mud, or broken grasses, or scratches on the bark of trees, to track down a marauding beast. Don't you *see*?" she demanded, irritated by the dull, puzzled look in his eyes. "By *investigating*. By being *investigators*."

"*In . . . vest . . .*" he began slowly, the way he did when she was trying to teach him a new word.

"*-igators*! Yes! It means 'crafty searchers.'"

He still looked puzzled.

"It comes from a Latin word. *Investigare*. To *track*," she said. "So *investigator* means 'he which tracketh.'"

Rob's eyes lit up. "Ah! Then *I* am an in-in—"

"Investigator, yes. And I, too. We will *both* be investigators. Only we will use *these* signs"—she pointed to the strand of twine, the hair, the burrs, the petal, and the grains of red soil—"to track down the person who did this to the kitten."

His face darkened. "Ah, yes," he said. "That is what I was minded to do. When I decided to preserve them."

"Good," she said. "Observing them was good. Preserving them was good. But now they must be *pondered.* And for that we need *other* skills."

She turned to the opposite side of the shed, where there was a much smaller pile of logs, with a crudely made desk box resting on top of it.

"Here, see," she said as she lifted the lid and drew out a large book with a decorated paperboard cover. "Pass me the scissors."

The first few pages were covered with her own neat printing. She'd started to write down the story of Rob's Indian captivity at his own dictation, as she'd done with the King Robert verses. She'd been hoping to use it, too, to help him practice his reading.

Knowing that, his eyes widened as she calmly took the scissors to the first page. All about his new Indian father and mother. About how they had selected the boy to replace their own son, killed at the same age by an English soldier.

Snip, snip—out it went.

She put the scissors to the second page. About the elderly woman in the tribe who'd started as a captive like him and was now the mother of three fierce braves. Running Deer—original name Mary Kelly. She'd been captured at the age of eighteen and could remember quite a lot of her native tongue. She'd befriended Rob so that she could practice it with him in long conversations.

Snip, snip—out *she* came.

Hester applied the scissors to the third page. (Rob was now more wide eyed than ever.) This was about how he'd told Running Deer of his grandfather's tales. Of the Scottish king, Robert, who had fought the English and driven them out of his country. About the methods that wily king had used, so much like the Indian methods employed against the white colonists.

Snip, snip. Out it came.

She put the scissors to the fourth page. About Running Deer realizing how interested the other Indians would be. How they loved to listen to such stories of bloody battles, cunningly fought. How she had him repeat them to the spellbound chiefs and elders, with herself interpreting.

Snip, snip. Out it went, too.

Hester hadn't even completed writing the fifth page. This was to have been about how the chiefs had connected Rob's true white-man name (they'd started calling him Blazing Scalp already) with the name of the great Scottish king. And how they figured he must have been a direct descendant of the hero who'd led his nation against the same foes as theirs.

She sighed. It was such a good story and would surely have encouraged him to read as no other would.

But first things first, she told herself. And—snip, snip—out *that* went, too.

Rob was now looking positively crestfallen to see his Indian boyhood being cut away like that.

"It is all right," she said, noticing his expression (and feeling rather pleased). She placed the loose pages in the desk. "We will return to them later. Meanwhile . . ."

She took out her quill and inkhorn. Then, very carefully, she wrote on the new first page:

"What does *that* say?" he asked as she blew on it to dry the ink.

"You would know if you had been more industrious this winter. . . . It says . . ." Touching each word, she read out the inscription.

His eyes narrowed. He may not have been very good at reading, but he never missed a suspicious detail.

"Investig*atrix*?" he murmured. "I thought you said—"

"Investig*ator*, yes. That was the male. This is the female. *She* who tracketh. *I*."

Now he looked hurt. "But—"

"With *your* help. Naturally. And here"—she flipped over the page—"we will begin to list all the signs we have so far noted."

5
The List

Under the heading "Signs," she wrote, in her best copperplate hand, *The Mark Itself,* repeating the words aloud, knowing he couldn't even begin to read what he called her "curly rippling writing."

Then she added the question: *Made by branding iron?*

"What think you?" she asked.

Rob shrugged. "I know of no brand like that cross on the creature's flank."

"Hmm!" Hester was frowning, flicking the tip of the quill against her nose. "Goodman Oldroyd branded his hogs last year. After disputing the ownership of one of them with Goody Pike."

"Yes," said Rob. "But it was with an O. 'Twas one of the first letters you taught me."

"Aye," she murmured thoughtfully. "And it was much better fashioned than this rude horrid cross. I doubt if Mr. Carter made *that* in his smithy."

"It was probably made in haste," said Rob. "For this one purpose. That is what *I* have thought."

Hester nodded. "I, too. And I have also thought that if we find that homemade iron, we will have found the person who used it so wickedly."

She wrote and read out the next item: *Length of thinne twine around the cat's neck.*

"I was just wondering . . . ," she murmured.

"What?"

"Could she have been caught in a snare?"

Rob picked up the piece of twine. "Only a child or a fool would use *this* kind of twine for a snare," he said.

"Well, what if it was a snare *made* by a child or a fool?"

"Even so, I think not. See this?" He pointed to the knot, just above where he'd cut the twine free. "This isn't the kind used for snares. This is a *firm* knot—one that holds, not slips. I think it was made as a collar to tether her by."

After she'd written, *3 burrs. Found in the cat's fur, with small blue petal and whyte hair of a dogge,* she looked up.

"I do not need for you to tell me the burrs came from a burdock plant, Rob. But which? Where?"

Rob shook his head. "Almost anywhere. Maybe even in Goody Willson's own garden. It is very common."

She'd feared as much. "But did you not tell me once that the Indians used to catch rabbits with burrs? By placing them in their tracks so they would stick to their paws and slow them?"

He grinned. "Aye. Sure. But not *these*. Burrs from a much bigger plant . . . these are from the common burdock. It *is* a sign, but no sign to be of much use to us.

Just as with the petal. That is from the patch of violets in Goody Willson's garden, I am sure."

"I see." She swallowed her disappointment. "And the hair? Think you she was attacked by a dog and left for dead? Before being found by the person who branded her?"

He smiled slightly and shook his head. "The wound on her head was no bite mark. 'Twas made by something hard and blunt—a stick or stone. And the hair was found in the fur under her belly. If there was a fight, then it is more like that she was the attacker, leaping atop the dog's back the way cats do."

"So—"

"But there is no other sign of a cat-and-dog fight. So all it tells us is that she has rested lately in some place where there has also been a dog with white hairs."

She sighed. That could have been almost anywhere, she guessed.

"I see," she said again, and resumed her writing: *Red dirt, found betwixt cat's toes.*

When she read it aloud, his face brightened. "Ah! Now that is *not* common. That came from higher ground. Beyond Mistress Brown's farther fields. Toward Morton's Mountain."

"Could she have strayed *that* far?"

"I doubt it," said Rob. "But she could a been *took* there."

Hester's eyes gleamed. "Good! That *is* a useful sign."

"Well," said Rob doubtfully, "it covers much ground. . . . What be this?"

Hester was rapidly writing again. When she'd finished, she read out the new item: *Rob's remark on first finding cat.*

"My remark?"

"Yes," she said. "When you stooped to it. You said, 'Strange!' . . . *How* 'strange'?"

"Why, her fur was dry."

She frowned, still not understanding. "Well?" she said. "Open to me this riddle. Why should the dryness of the creature's fur be so strange?"

"Because the stone on which she lay, underneath and all around her, was *wet.* That means—"

"Enough!" She was excited now. "I see! She must have been placed there *after* the thunderstorm that came in the middle of the lecture."

"Just so," said Rob gravely.

She wrote, reading it aloud, *Cat's fur dry. Therefore placed there by person not attending lecture.*

"That could prove a *very* important sign," she said. "I'd have thought almost everyone in town was at that lecture, it was so crowded."

"Save one, at least. One who *never* enters the meetinghouse."

"Who—ah! You mean Eben?"

"Yes," he said.

"But he only comes to eavesdrop," said Hester. " 'They may exclude me from the building, but they cannot keep me from hearing the word of God!' He is always saying that."

"I know," said Rob.

"And why would *he* do such a thing to the cat?" she said. "I know he's crazy, but . . . well . . ." She shrugged.

"Maybe in the course of our investigations we will hap upon some other sign that *will* point to him."

"I do not think so," Rob said.

He spoke with such certainty that she looked hard at him.

"Why not?"

"Because when I am tracking I always close my eyes and try to see a picture of the prey. And I cannot see Eben doing this thing."

She suppressed a smile. "We must seek the exact *facts*, Rob," she said. "Not imaginings."

He looked angry for an instant—stung. Then he said quietly, "Do you still have my red crayon stick?"

She frowned. The red crayon was what he used for his own attempts at printing the alphabet on paper, his use of the quill having been disastrous for blots and smudges.

"Yes . . . I think so." She lifted the desk lid. "Why?"

"Then find it for me, pray. There is one sign that is chiefest of all."

"Uh . . . which?" she asked, handing him the crayon.

"This," he said, going across to the cat. "The mark. We need to make a true picture of it."

"But why?" she asked. "I have already writ it down."

"Yes." He picked up the piece of twine and bent over the cat. "But if we should find the tool that made the mark, we may need to match it."

"Well, but the mark will not go from the kitten's flesh until the fur be grown over it again," she said.

"If the cat lives, yes," he said. "But if it dies we will have to bury it or burn it. Before it stinks. And then we will have no true match."

It was brutal, but it made sense.

"Very well," she said. "It is a wise precaution, I suppose."

She watched as he carefully measured each leg of the cross with the piece of twine and reproduced it in crayon, muttering "exact *facts*" with every stroke. And in the end she had to admit that *she* could never have made such an accurate picture of the mark.

"Very *good!*" she murmured, glancing from cat to drawing and back again.

Then she wrote under it, *A true likeness of the mark made in the cat's fur.*

"What does that say?" he asked.

She told him.

"Then add this," he said, with a glint of triumph. "Add 'on its right-hand flank between the ham and the collarbone.' 'Twill be more *exact*. When tracking in the woods, the *position* of a sign can tell you as much as its appearance."

She grunted and began to write. He could certainly be a fast learner when he put his mind to it, she was thinking.

Then there was a knock on the door.

6
Mistress Brown's Warning

It was Nell.

When she stepped inside, her bright brown eyes were everywhere. On the book, on the sheet of paper, on the quill in Hester's hand, on the crayon in Rob's. As usual when she came upon the two of them alone, she looked somewhat suspicious. Obviously she still found it hard to trust someone she continued to think of as a savage—especially with her favorite, Hester.

But then she saw the cat, and her face softened.

"Ai! Bless its little soul!" she crooned. "Will it mend, lad?"

Before Rob could reply, Hester said, "If it is allowed to recover in peace and warmth and with loving care."

There was a gentle glow in Nell's eyes as she said, "Well, I am sure *you* will give it that, my bird!"

Hester bit on her lower lip and replied in a sad voice, "I truly would, Nell. If my aunt would allow us to have it in the house. But she has forbid it."

"And my grandmother—" Rob began.

"I know, lad," Nell said grimly. "She is one of they

who is convinced it be a witch's familiar. I heard her saying so outside the meetinghouse."

Hester took a deep breath. "I suppose Goody Willson herself is not yet fit to look after it?"

"Not even to see it," said Nell, grimmer than ever. "In the state she herself be in, she, too, is in need of all the peace and care she can get just now." Nell scowled. "Aye, and all the protection she can get!"

Hester had gotten very quiet. She looked up almost shyly and said, "*You* do not believe Goody Willson a witch and the kitten her familiar, do you, Nell?"

"Of course not, child!" said the woman. "Shame on thee for ever asking! I leave such dafters' drivel to they who have nothing better to do."

"Nor Mistress Brown?" said Hester. "*She* doesn't believe—?"

"Ha! You know as well as I, child, *her* views on such matters! She has often enough spoke about—" Suddenly Nell stopped. Then a slow grin began to spread across her face. "Ah-ha, Madam Slyboots! I begin to make out thy meaning! You would like *us* to provide an infirmary for the kitling! Well ..." She looked down at it with pity. Then, frowning, she turned to Rob. "Has it eaten yet?"

Rob shook his head. "No. Only a little water. Not until tomorrow should it partake of anything more nourishing. If it *will*."

Hester's heart gave a little leap. He couldn't have said anything more likely to arouse Nell's active support.

"Oh, I trow it *will*!" the good woman said scornfully. The cat now had one eye open again, seeming to gaze back at her as hopefully as Hester was feeling. "We will see what she says to a dib of fresh cream from the tip of her old Nell's little finger.... Eh, my lamb?" she murmured, addressing the cat itself.

"Anyway," said Nell, turning to Hester, "here we be, chatting like old hens, and I have come to summon you to Mistress Brown. She wishes urgently to speak with you about the afternoon's sorry events."

"Both of us?" asked Hester.

"Aye," said Nell, with a barely disguised glance of disapproval at Rob. Then she brightened up. "And we can take along this little soul"—she was already wrapping her shawl closer—"before it perishes in these drafts.... I have thought mayhap to use what my mistress calls her library. What she had me turn into a winter schoolroom for you both." She sniffed. "Heaven knows, it's been little enough used as *that,* these last months."

Hester gave Rob a quick, gleeful nudge as he picked up the tray and they got ready to follow Nell.

"You *see!*" she whispered. "The creature *will* live now!"

"Goody Willson be in a very evil case!" said Mistress Brown, shaking her head in that trembly way of hers. "We *all* be in an evil case if this should go on unchecked."

The cat had been installed in the warm schoolroom-library, still nestling on the black cap. Now, as Rob sat with a steaming mug of lemon-mint tea in one hand, he was holding a green woolen replacement cap in the other. Mistress Brown had lent it to him out of the large stock of clothing she always kept by for orphans and others in need. "So that you needn't disturb the poor creature," she had said.

Nell was still with the invalid. No doubt she was already defying "doctor's" orders and trying to tempt it with smears of cream. She will if *I* know her, Hester was thinking.

Then she quickly quelled a smile as she noted the anxiety in Mistress Brown's eyes—small, bright, and birdlike under the frilly white cap.

Despite the dancing flames of the log fire, the old lady was cocooned, frail and tiny, in layers of shawls and blankets. Sometimes it was hard to believe she had built up the largest holding of farmland in Willow Bend, running it with no kinsman to help her for the past thirty years, ever since her brother's death. With no sons or daughters either. But she'd given shelter and help to numerous godchildren in her time—mainly orphans. Even Mr. Lawson, the magistrate, had been one of these.

That was why, with so many people in the village who had cause to be grateful to Mistress Brown and who respected her deeply, it seemed strange that she herself should be so anxious.

But she obviously was.

"At my age it is easy to drift off into the past and speak ramblingly of other times," she was saying now. "I know *I* do it on occasion."

Hester shook her head, wanting to be kind, but knowing that what Mistress Brown said was true.

"Ah yes, child, I do!" said the old lady. "Haven't I

sometimes talked of dragons and castles back in old England? As if I had fought with them and lived in them?"

"Well . . ."

"Old women do prate of such fancies. 'Tis only natural." Mistress Brown's trembling increased. "But if this Salem madness takes hold here, all such ramblings will be claimed as proof of witchery. And not only that. Every bodily blemish that comes with age. Every mole and sprout of hair upon the cheek—all these will be spoken of by some as witch marks."

"Oh, but Mistress Brown," said Hester, "a woman of your standing would never be accused!"

"It makes no difference," said the old lady. "Luke Lawson tells me that even the mother-in-law of Judge Corwin of Salem is being mentioned. Aye, even Mistress Margaret Thacher. Her being kin to a judge will not save her if this goes on!"

Rob grunted angrily. Hester wondered if he was thinking of what would surely have happened to any Indian who dared to make such accusations against the mother of one of the chiefs.

Mistress Brown, too, seemed to have been reading something of his thoughts.

"'Tis not only the old women who are in danger," she said. "Anyone, male or female, young or old, with a birthmark or a defect—a squint, a harelip, a clubfoot—these things also can be turned into evidence"—she paused, wheezing—"by those bent on crying out some innocent as a witch." She was getting very tired. Her lips were quite blue.

"Mistress Brown," Hester said gently, "don't you think you should—?"

The old lady was waving a thin, freckled hand. "Even you, child, with hair of your color. And yours, young man. I have lived through such times before and, believe me, young women have been put to death for—for having red hair. And not just the color. Some maids have been condemned merely for the habit of tossing their hair in defiance. . . . Even that has been called a witch sign."

Hester wondered if this would be a good time to mention the signs that she and Rob had decided to investigate.

But the old lady was continuing. "So the mark of a cross upon the cat . . ." She shook her head. "Poor Goody Willson!"

Goody Willson was another of Mistress Brown's waifs and strays, someone she'd taken under her wing ever since Jabez Willson had run off to Boston with another woman. Mistress Brown looked so distressed just then that Hester decided to tell her of the plan right away.

As it was outlined, the old lady seemed to gather strength.

"Good!" she said when Hester was through. "Very good!" Then she pursed her lips. "And know *this*. I will be here to give thee every assistance. Consider thy regular jobs for me to be suspended forthwith. Rob—thy work in the garden, the fencing of the west meadow. You, my pet—the quilting I was about to set you to. Leave such matters until after you track the rascal down. . . . However long it take. . . . Though—though I pray to God it will not be long. For the sake of Goody Willson and all of us who—"

There was a sudden frantic knocking at an outer door.

"Whoever is this?" murmured the old lady.

Then they heard voices.

"They are *here*, Mistress Bidgood," Nell was saying. "Pray come in. . . ." As she was ushered in, Aunt Elizabeth looked very flustered.

"Good evening, Mistress Brown," she said with a strained smile. Then, turning to Hester and Rob, she said angrily, "Oh, you naughts! Why didst you not tell me you was coming here?"

"The fault is mine, Elizabeth," said Mistress Brown. "I kept them talking. . . . Nell, bring Mistress Bidgood a glass of canary. She looks in need of it."

"Oh, no!" Aunt Elizabeth feebly protested. "But . . . well . . . for my stomach's sake, just a little, then. It do be churned up, I confess. With fright," she added, frowning at Hester.

"Fright?" said Mistress Brown. "Nay!"

"Oh, yes, Mistress Brown!" said the invalid. "In *my* state of health—thank you, Nell." She took a sip of the wine. "In my state, even the sudden sight of a mouse can bring on the vapors. . . ." Another sip. "So when I went to the shed to call Hester in to supper and found it in darkness, and them gone, the cat and all . . ." She took a full gulp this time. "Well, then I thought for sure it must a been Satan hisself. He must a been to claim his own, that creature of Goody Willson's, and took them with him for hostages."

A snort issued from Mistress Brown's blue lips. "Come, Elizabeth! Such things don't happen outside the old tales!"

"Ai, but they do, Mistress Brown!" said Aunt Elizabeth. "Begging your pardon, but they do! Such things are happening elsewhere every day in the colony. And that gray creature do be a witch's familiar. The stamp of God upon its side sayeth so!"

"Nonsense!" said Mistress Brown. Then she added, "Finish your wine, Elizabeth, and call for Nell. 'Tis time for me to retire."

She spoke wearily, but the look in her eyes as she glanced at Hester and Rob was wakeful enough. Grimly wakeful. It said, as plainly as if she'd spoken the words aloud, There. You see. It will take proof positive to convince such people that it was a real flesh-and-bone human being who did this evil thing. Go find that person!

7
Branding Irons:
An Expert's Opinion

The next morning, after looking in on the invalid, Hester felt full of hope.

The cat seemed well settled. They'd left it licking the black tip of its tail, which Nell was keeping white with cream. It was still lying on Rob's cap. It hadn't yet tried any of the food in an array of saucers all around it. "But she *will* before long," said Nell, adding proudly, "And she has used the tray of sawdust, with my help to lift her on and off it. She *asked* me to!"

Outside, the morning itself appeared radiant with the promise of renewed life. It wasn't as cold and cloudy as the day before. The sun flashed and glinted on pools in the waterlogged fields. The sky was filled with birds: wild geese flying in small strands and broken skeins in all directions, with blackbirds and others in huge flocks, rising and curling like smoke. Yes, it was a splendid day for tracking, Hester thought. Even the new kind they were now embarking upon.

But when they left the well-graveled farm road and entered the main street, Hester's mood changed. It was as muddy here as ever, and Hester *hated* mud. It was all right for boys and men. Rob was wearing his everyday clothes—the loose tunic, fringed buckskin leggings, moccasins—but even wearing his Sunday suit he'd have been better off than she was in this slabby ooze. With every other step, she was having to hitch her long skirts.

"What is troubling you?" Rob asked.

"Mud. I loathe it!"

"But why?" he said. "No mud, no thaw. No thaw, no spring."

She gave him an anxious sidelong glance. He had that wistful look as he gazed up at the sky, as if he'd have loved to be stalking some of those geese when they lit on the temporary lagoons in the fields.

She decided to remind him of the tracking he'd been so enthusiastic about the previous afternoon. "The signs we are investigating . . . ," she murmured.

"Yes?"

"*They* are like these stepping stones."

"Oh?" He looked at her. Anything sounding like a riddle always interested him.

"Yes," she said. "And one by one the signs will lead us out of the mire of this wicked matter to discover the true culprit. And the—*Oh!*"

She'd been so wrapped-up in her words that she missed one of the stones and slid on the mud.

He put out a hand to steady her, but she shook it off. There were people about, and she was really angry now.

"The disgusting stuff!" she muttered, hitching her skirts high again as she led the way across the street to the smithy, which they'd already chosen as the first point of their inquiry.

But she wasn't the only one disgusted.

"*Tsk!*" The cluck of disapproval came from a woman approaching from the opposite side. It was Goody Pierce. "Showing all thy legs! Lower thy skirts, wench!"

Hester gave her head a defiant toss and looked away. A year ago—even six months ago—she would have blushed and mumbled an apology. But not now. Not today. Some of these elders were far too concerned over such trifles. Evil, real evil, was stalking and striking all around them, and they didn't seem to be able to recognize it.

"Wanton little hussy!" the woman called out.

Hester tossed her head again—then immediately wished she hadn't, remembering too late Mistress Brown's words about witch signs.

"Have a care, Hester!" Rob whispered. "The widow Pierce be a vicious tattletale."

"Yes, I know," she murmured. "But come along. The sooner we bottom this mystery, the sooner we'll all be out of danger from such malicious tongues as hers."

Enoch Carter, the blacksmith, was hammering a plowshare into better shape. He was short but broad, barrel-like. Although quite old, he was still muscular and powerful. He had a bushy white beard and a bald head, brown and freckled, with small blue scars. They'd been made by flying flakes of hot metal, according to what he'd once told Hester. She'd been a lot younger then. She smiled grimly now, wondering if the scars would be counted as witch marks by the foolish or spiteful.

"If you've come about Mistress Brown's plowshares," he said, still hammering, "tell her I'm working on them. Tell her everybody be clamoring all at once to have their tools readied for the plowing and planting."

"Yes, Mr. Carter," Hester said. "But we've really come to ask about branding irons."

He raised his bristly black eyebrows. "Have ye now?" he said, pausing in his hammering.

"Yes. Have you made any lately?"

The smith shook his head. "There be little call for such implements nowadays, my lass. Now, in my father's time, when it was the custom to brand criminals and such—*M* for your murderer, *L* for your liar, *T* for your thief, *H* for your heretic, and so on—blacksmiths was kept busy. . . ."

He didn't seem to notice Hester's disappointment. He chuckled before continuing, "I still remember the vexation it caused my father to make a *B* for *blasphemer*. Heh! He came pretty close to blaspheming hisself as he wrassled with they wriggly curves and bends."

Rob grinned. "'Tis hard enough making that letter with a quill!"

The old man laughed. "Thou'st said it, lad! Even a *P* for *perjurer* was tricksy enough. I remember trying to make one for him as an apprentice piece. It came out more like a *D*. ''Twill do if they ever get around to branding debtors,' he said. Heh! It may still be seen, hanging by the tavern fireplace with the other irons."

Hester suddenly stiffened. "Oh?"

"Yes," said Mr. Carter. "When their use was discontinued in the jail, Ezra Cleary brought them into the tavern. He thought to put them to mulling ale and wine on frosty nights. But Magistrate Lawson said it would be a mockery of matters gravely serious."

"But you—"

"So Ezra had to go back to mulling the reg'lar way. With a red-hot poker."

"But you said they still hang there?" Hester quickly interposed.

"Aye. In the chimney corner. But only as curiosities, gathering dust. No one takes much note of them anymore."

Hester caught her breath. Then: "Was—*is* there a cross—an *X*—among them?"

The smith's eyes twinkled. "Nay, lass! And they say you're such a scholar, too! What sin or crime would there be that starts with an *X*?"

Quick-minded, her pride stung (and in front of her prize pupil, too!), Hester was about to say *extortion,* but remembered in time that it began with an *E.*

"There is definitely no *X* iron, then?" she murmured.

Mr. Carter looked at her curiously. "I have already said it."

"And no one has asked you to make one lately?" she persisted. "After all, you did make an *O* to brand Mr. Oldroyd's hogs with last year. Didn't you?"

"Aye, that I did," said the smith. "I was hoping others would follow his lead, but they haven't. If more folk would brand their sheep and kine, there'd be fewer disputes."

He resumed his hammering. Then he stopped as if

he'd had a new thought. "A cross, you say?" But he was grinning. "He would have to be some kind of heathen or fool, wouldn't he, to ask for such a shape? After the minister's great sermon last year?"

"About *branding irons*?" asked Hester, puzzled.

"Nay! About the use of a cross by the unlettered for making their marks when signing documents. Very nigh blasphemous, he called it."

Hester remembered Mr. Phipps's sermon now. How he'd called on people either to learn to write their names, or at least to make some special mark other than a cross.

"So after *that*," the old man concluded, "who would dare use a cross for branding upon the arses of their beasts?"

Disappointed, the investigators moved on toward the next place. This was to have been Goody Willson's yard, but as they were about to pass Cleary's tavern on the way, Hester stopped.

"Perhaps we'd best check on whether there is an *X* iron among the others in there, after all," she said. "Who knows? Mr. Carter may have misremembered."

A rumble of voices was coming from inside.

"Why don't you go in and make sure, Rob?"

"But—"

"Pretend you're looking to see if one of Mistress Brown's field hands be in there. I'll remain outside."

She didn't have to wait long.

When he came out, his eyes were burning.

"Well?" she said.

"There was no *X* among them," he growled.

"Oh, well," she said, "it's nothing to get angry about."

"I am not angry about that. 'Tis Mr. Cleary who hath angered me."

"Why?"

"Insolent as his son!" muttered Rob. "Persisting in calling me an Indian! Said he refused to serve Indians with liquor."

She felt her chin recoil in shock. "Did you *call* for some?"

"Of course not! He said it before I had the chance to say about looking for someone."

"But you *did* check the irons?"

"Yes. I have already told you.... Huh! As if any Indian would think of drinking liquor when he was out hunting! ... Where did you say next?"

Hester was glad to see him so keen to get back on the scent. "Goody Willson's yard," she said. "Who knows what signs we might find there?"

8
Violets, Bad Smells, and Snares: Further Expert Opinion

As they drew near to Goody Willson's house, Rob said, "Should we tell her how well the cat is faring?"

"No," said Hester. "It would cheer her perhaps, but remember what Nell told us. The poor woman is keeping to her bed. She's still half out of her mind with bewilderment. We must—"

"Huh!" grunted Rob. "Thieves have been at work!"

Goody Willson's house was one of the smaller, meaner dwellings in back of the main street, beyond the cemetery. It had a small front yard, fenced in with a lilac hedge, which was sprouting its first leaves. There was a plot of brown grass where Goody Willson used to tether a goat, but the animal had died of old age during the winter. Unable to afford another, she had decided to have the grass dug over and grow vegetables there instead. Mistress Brown had promised to send one of her hands to do the digging come spring, and some weeks ago had had a load of horse dung delivered in readiness. Rob himself had helped cart it there.

It was this, piled tidily inside the hedge near the gate, that he was glaring at now.

There seemed to be only half of it left. "Look!" he said. "See how it gleams and glistens afresh where it has been dug into!"

"Already!" said Hester. "As soon as they heard the poor woman was sick in bed!"

"Aye," murmured Rob grimly, beginning to step forward. "And there appears to be another thief at work even now."

There was a holly bush at the corner of the house. Beyond this, along the side, there was a patch of wild violets. These were acknowledged to be the earliest and sweetest for miles around, and there were some who whispered that this was yet another sign of Goody Willson's being in league with the devil.

Stealthily, Hester followed Rob past the holly screen. Then they both burst in on the figure crouching over the withered grass, where the violets were already shyly blooming.

"Oh, it's *you*, Peacemaker Cleary!" Hester said. "What are you doing?"

There was a small burlap sack on the ground at his side. It was unfolded, ready to be filled.

After giving them one startled look, Cleary turned back to the flowers. "What doth it look like?" he muttered, plucking clumsily at the patch. "I'm gathering them for Goody Pierce. For her candied violets."

Goody Pierce was famous for making these every year, just after sugaring time. Maybe this was where the woman had been coming from earlier, out on the street,

Hester thought. After pointing the violets out to Peace-maker and asking Goody Willson's permission.

Then Hester frowned. Somehow she couldn't imagine the malicious busybody asking any such favor from someone she was known to despise.

"Has Goody Willson given you leave to pick them?" she asked.

Peacemaker Cleary hesitated. "Who needs a witch's leave?" he muttered.

Hester flared. "Then get out! You're trespassing on her property!"

The lopsided sneer squirmed across the boy's face. "Witches *have* no property!"

"She has not been tried and proved a witch!" said Hester. "Nor will she be. So get out, or I will report this to Magistrate Lawson!"

The naming of this authority had its usual effect on Cleary. He scowled, but got to his feet. He flung a handful of grass and violets at Hester in his rage.

Then, snatching up his nearly empty sack, he began to slink toward the gate, giving Rob a walleyed glare. "Thou'rt only jealous because Goody Pierce will not buy her violets from *thee*!" he snarled.

"Aye," said Rob, quite unmoved. "Because I refuse to steal the earliest and biggest from other people's yards. And because she hasn't the wit to know that some of the wilder violets contain much better medicine."

"Medicine!" sneered Peacemaker. "A pox on thy Indian medicine! Son of a squaw!"

Then Rob *did* move. "You called me that yesterday, son of a pig-faced tapster!" he growled, covering the ground in two or three strides.

Too late, Cleary turned to run. Rob was already grabbing him by the scruff of the neck and the loose cloth of his britches.

"Hoy!" cried Cleary—but by then he'd been tossed sprawling, slap-splash, onto the freshly plundered manure heap.

Hester cast an anxious glance at an upper window, where she'd seen a movement. But it was only a pair of phoebe birds fluttering to their nest under the eaves. She hoped Goody Willson slept in the back and wouldn't be too disturbed, for now there was somewhat of an uproar, as Peacemaker Cleary staggered off, sobbing and cursing. Peals of laughter were arising from a bunch of passing boys. Unhappily for Peacemaker, they were lads of nearly his own age, not the very small ones he tended to lord it over.

"That was good to see, Rob!" said one, after wiping his eyes.

"Aye, he asked to be dealt with so," added another.

"Now mayhap he will *have* to take a tubbing!" said a third.

"Think so?" said the first. "*I* think the horse muck will have much *improved* his smell!"

Rob was frowning thoughtfully. "Never heed *him*," he said, taking something from his pocket. "Have any of you been using twine like this of late? Say for your snares?"

It was the strand from the cat's neck.

They crowded around. Rob was watching their faces keenly.

"Nay," said one boy. "That be too thick. *I* use twisted horsehair. The way you showed us."

"Me, too."

"And I."

"Good!" said Rob. "And you minded what else I said?"

"About using gloves to set it? So the rabbits don't catch our scent? Aye. But I *still* haven't caught nothing yet."

"Nor I."

"Me either."

"You will." Rob put the twine back into his pocket, then hesitated. "Hath yon *Cleary* been setting snares?"

"Not he!" said the chief spokesman. "He be too busy gathering herbs."

"Aye," said another. "He seeks to steal thy trade, Rob. We've heard him boasting of it. By charging the good-wives less than you."

"But don't worry," said the first. "There be some who wouldn't have his herbs *given* them."

"They say he don't know one root from another," the third chimed in. "Not since Goody Benson took something he said would soothe her sore throat and she found herself running to the privy twenty times in one day!"

As the boys went off, roaring with laughter again, Hester turned to Rob. *She* wasn't laughing. "Why didn't you ask them if they'd used such twine for *other* purposes lately?"

"There was no need," he said. "I was watching their faces when I showed them the scrap. Had one of them used it for tethering the cat, his guilt would have shown. His unease, anyway."

She found herself smiling. She was beginning to realize just how crafty a searcher he was.

"That was a very cunning way of finding out!" she said.

"Huh!" he grunted. "What did you expect? That I should subject them to Indian tortures to discover the truth?"

Hester blushed. Sometimes she wasn't sure when he was serious and when he was making sport of her.

9
The Country of the Red Earth

"We have learned one thing, anyway," said Hester as they watched the boys out of sight. "Most likely the cat was not taken from its own yard."

"Why not?"

"The culprit would not have dared, lest he be seen," she said.

"Huh! Someone dared to steal the manure," said Rob. "And Peacemaker Cleary dared to pick the violets."

"Ah, yes!" said Hester. "*Today.* When Goody Willson is known to be helpless in bed. But yesterday morning, before all this happened, she was well enough."

He still looked doubtful.

"So in *my* opinion," Hester went on, "the cat was most like to have been picked up somewhere outside the yard. And not here but in back, where there are only fields and but few passersby."

Rob nodded slowly. "'Twould be where the creature *would* make short forays from the house," he said.

But having used her logic to suggest where to look

next, Hester had to leave it to his more practical skills when it came to searching the area.

A path ran along the edge of the field, close to the backyards, and it did look promising at first. Near to the fences and ragged hedges were clumps of rough vegetation: withered grass, briers, and brambles. Some were littered with rotting garbage that must have been a great attraction to rats and mice (she lifted her skirts higher at the thought), and therefore of equally great interest to any cat. There was even a patch where some violets were beginning to flower—smaller and sparser than Goody Willson's.

"He could have picked some *here,*" murmured Rob. "They would have been good enough."

But it was the path itself that most interested him. It was muddy, but not as bad as in parts of the streets. People from the nearby houses sometimes used it, and there were plenty of clear human footprints, as well as those of dogs, raccoons, and cats of various sizes, according to Rob. He even claimed to recognize some likely to have been made by Goody Willson's cat.

"But that is not what I am looking for," he said, frowning down.

"What then?" said Hester, keeping well away from a garbage-strewn bramble bush, from which she thought she'd heard a faint rustling.

"A place where the prints of a human and those of a cat converge. Where the human tracks stop and sink in deeper at the toes, and the cat's back paws scrabbled the mud."

"Why? What would *that* tell you?" she asked.

"Of someone bending down and snatching the creature up," he said. "Then, by studying those shoe prints more closely, we might be able to track down the owner. But"—he kicked at a stray cabbage stalk—"there is no such sign."

For all his own disappointment, Hester gave him a glance of admiration mixed with envy. Even if she'd identified such marks, she'd never have been able to interpret them so vividly.

"Anyway," said Rob, "this be dark earth, not the red that I found between the cat's toes."

"Yes," she murmured. "Didn't you say it came from higher ground?"

"Aye." He glanced at the sun. "But to continue our search in those parts will take hours. Maybe even days. We must leave it until after we've eaten our nooning."

Hester wasn't reluctant to leave. The strengthening sun was beginning to raise a stench from the garbage. That and the smell of privies was becoming much too powerful for comfort.

Straight after the meal, they headed for what Rob called "the country of the red earth," and they hadn't gone far along the track that separated Mistress Brown's property from Jacob Peabody's before they reached it. The soil in the fields here, still stippled and streaked with snow in places, changed abruptly from a blackish gray to reddish purple. "And it is the same in there, too," Rob said, when the cultivated land gave way to trees. "So that is where we will begin our search."

"Not out here?" she asked, glancing at the fields.

"No," he said. "It was a skulking, sneaking deed. One that would only be done where there was plenty of cover and where smoke from the fire would not attract attention in the village."

Hester looked doubtful. "But the forest stretches for miles!"

"Aye. But there be limits," he said. "To the east, beyond half a mile, it becomes my grandfather's property. The evildoer would not have wished to attract *his* attention with a fire. Nor any of his men's. They are all very wary of the dangers of chance fires in there."

She looked at him curiously, alert for signs that had nothing to do with the cat now.

Old Mr. MacGregor had built up a thriving business in timber—felling trees, planting new ones, selling some logs for fuel and others for turning into planks or barrel staves or, more and more, fencing materials. When Rob had first been freed, the youth had expressed his preference for setting to work in this trade at once.

But his grandfather wouldn't hear of it. "Nay, laddie! I havena redeemed you with a prince's ransom only to turn ye inta a common forester. What I want for *you* is that ye learn yer letters and then go on to that fine Harvard College they've got up in Boston. That's where they'll make something of you that'll carry some weight in the coming century. Like a lawyer, say."

That was when Mr. MacGregor turned and winked at Hester, who'd been summoned to that first interview in Mistress Brown's parlor.

"So mark well what this canny young lass teaches you. Aye—and pay heed to the manners with which this good lady conducts her household. Then you'll be full fitted for starting on a gentleman's profession."

Rob had never seemed to be thrilled at such a prospect, and Hester had wondered lately if it hadn't added to his growing hankering for the wider freedoms of Indian life.

But he wasn't showing any signs of it now. All he seemed to have in mind was the search.

"And a little higher," he was saying, "to the northeast, is where old Eben has his hut. The evildoer wouldn't want to attract *his* attention neither."

"Unless old Eben *was* the evildoer."

"I have said already I do not picture him as that," Rob stated firmly.

She shrugged. She still wasn't convinced about the hermit's innocence, but since the morning her faith in Rob's picturing had grown some.

It strengthened even more as he went on.

"So from here to about five hundred paces into the trees we will conduct our search. Inspecting every sheltered hollow and glade. Back and forth, working our way higher."

"But what—?"

"And we will all the time be looking for these signs." He counted them off on his fingers. "The remains of a fire. A nearby stump or sapling to which the other end of the tether might have been tied. A bloodied rock, or stick maybe. And—who knows?—haply the branding iron itself."

Given such concrete details, she found her sense of hopelessness melting and she followed him eagerly along deer tracks, up and down hollows, and across fast-flowing creeks, swollen since the thaw. Squirrels sometimes scolded them, sometimes a jay screeched, but for the most part they searched in silence—save for the sudden scream that escaped her when she saw a bush stir not more than six feet away and she thought she caught a glimpse of a ghostlike face.

"What is it?" said Rob, turning swiftly.

"In—in there . . ." She peered into the dense mass of twigs, then shook her head. "'Tis nothing. I thought—I thought it was a bear maybe."

Suddenly Rob grinned. He was looking at another dense bush close to the first. "Good afternoon, Mr. Cranshaw!" he said. "Well met! I wonder if—"

But Crazy Eben was in no mood for polite gossip. With a grunt, he rose to his full height, turned, and stalked off. He was wearing a raccoon-skin hat and a coat made of a mixture of pelts, roughly stitched tgether.

"Have you seen the remains of a fire in these parts?" Rob called after him.

"Only the flames of the great fire to come, leaping and devouring all that be around, save me and yon sweet lass!" replied the hermit without stopping.

Hester felt her cheeks redden. He was always talking like that. About the appointment he and she would keep on top of Morton's Mountain on the eve of the new century, when together they'd watch the rest of the world burn to a cinder.

She shuddered at the thought of the madman's getting so close without being heard. And she still had doubts about his innocence.

But as the next hour or so went by, she began to re-gret the old man hadn't stayed to be questioned more narrowly. For their search was proving fruitless. They came across various interesting—and sometimes rather alarming—things. Like the antlers of a stag, the bones of a fawn (picked clean), and a flint arrowhead attached to a rotting wooden shaft, which Rob identified as Mo-hawk and no more than three or four years old. She even recognized the very sassafras tree from which he had plucked a leaf stalk early last summer and invited her to chew on for its special spicy flavor. In return she had shown him the shape of the letter *A*, by tearing off the central lobe of one of its leaves.

But no charred remains of a fire.

No bloodstained rock or stick.

And certainly no discarded branding iron.

And why should there be? The nagging thought per-sisted. If Eben had himself committed that deed, he'd have done it in the secrecy of his own hut, wouldn't he?

When they reached the edge of the forest again, the sun was sinking low in the sky.

"The light is getting too dim to be searching in there any longer today," Rob said. "There *is* one other place, not among the trees, that has come to my mind. But even there it will soon not be light enough."

"Where?"

"The Morton homestead."

Hester shuddered again, this time at the thought of the crumbling ruin in a clearing beyond the Brown and Peabody fields. It had a reputation for being haunted.

"Let's go back," she said. "It *is* getting late, and we can renew our search first thing in the morning."

Looking down from the field track onto the huddle of dwellings with wisps of blue smoke rising slowly into the air, Hester felt glad to be returning. Willow Bend still seemed to offer peace and safety when compared to the shadowy forest and the grimness of such blighted ruins as the Morton place. And when they entered the streets, the feeling of security was strengthened by the voices of little children, playing out in the magical rose-and-purple light of the afterglow.

Yes, *magical,* she thought as they drew near to one such group on the lawn in front of the manse, not far from the sycamore tree—its fat yellow buds seeming to shine a deeper gold in that light.

"Hester! Hester! Come look at our poppets!" one of the children called out.

Hester smiled. There were four of them. Rebecca Phipps, Mercy Carter (the blacksmith's granddaughter), and Mary and Elizabeth Parkin. Rebecca's poppet was a rather fine rag doll, but the others were made out of coarser materials—some cunningly twisted cornstalks, a gnarled root, even a twig from the sycamore—all tricked out with strips of cloth that had obviously come from Mistress Phipps's basket, lying on the ground at the side of the well.

"But what are you *doing* with them?" Hester asked, still smiling.

They laughed and capered with glee while Rebecca's young pet spaniel, Captain, frisked in and out between their feet—a gold-and-white bundle of fun with flapping ears and quivering tail.

"Testing them!" said Mercy Carter, plunging her

cornstalk poppet into the well bucket and holding it down, seemingly unconcerned that she was getting her sleeve as wet as the creature's rags. "See! She floats!" she screamed joyously, releasing it, with Captain's yapping echoing her screams.

"Pricking them!" said Rebecca, thrusting a needle into her doll's soft belly.

"Hanging them!" said Mary Parkin, laughing, tying hers by the neck to the uptilted well sweep with a piece of red knitting yarn.

"Aye!" said her sister with a sly smile, doing the same with her poppet. "They be witches!"

"That—that is not a very pretty game!" Hester whispered, turning to go.

Their laughter only got louder. They really meant no harm, she was sure. To them it was a mere game. But—

"Are you feeling well?" she heard Rob say.

This time she didn't shake his hand off her arm. Instead, she gently detached it and forced a smile.

" 'Tis nothing," she murmured. "My head was whimming it about for a moment. I'm all right now."

What she didn't say was that her dizziness had come on at the sight of Elizabeth Parkin's doll dangling from the well sweep, and her realizing that its wild and tangled hair had been made from the same yarn as the noose around its neck.

Red yarn for a red-haired witch . . .

10
The Scene of the Evil Deed

They visited the Morton place early the next morning.

The remains of the stone chimney stack loomed eerily in the mist as they stood and gazed at it across the stretch of long, withered grass, now drenched and beaded with heavy dew. Hester tried to picture it as it must have been once, but it was impossible. The air of desolation was too strong.

Besides the chimney stack, all that remained of the homestead were low mounds that marked the foundations of what had been a mainly wooden building. It was open to the sky now. The thatched roof must have been the first to go up in flames. And there wasn't anything at all to show where the outer stockade of logs had been—the family's main defense against marauders.

Hester knew these details only from hearsay. It was now almost twenty years since the farm had been attacked by an Indian war party and the whole Morton family had been massacred: father, mother, three sons, and two daughters.

"They say 'tis haunted by the ghosts of the Mortons,"

Hester murmured, feeling reluctant to go any closer.

"Aye, very likely," said Rob. "And haunted by Indian braves, too, no doubt."

"Oh?" said Hester. She'd heard about the marauders losing some men, but hadn't thought of them returning as ghosts.

"Surely!" said Rob. "If dead white people sometimes leave their ghosts behind, why not Indians?" He grinned. "Methinks there be one up yonder even now. Scouting out before the raid, as he did all those years ago. Drawing his ghostly bow on us."

Hester looked up at the rising ground to their right, but saw nothing except slowly swirling mist. She shivered despite the unseasonal mugginess of the air.

"I wish you would not make such jokes," she said.

"I am not joking," said Rob. "We *are* being spied upon. But 'tis no Narraganset or Pequot ghost. It is a flesh-and-blood admirer of yours—if you can call old Eben flesh and blood."

"Admirer!"

"Anyway, pay no heed," said Rob. "We haven't come to investigate *him*!"

As they slowly made their way toward the ruin, with Rob alert for signs of anyone else who'd passed that way recently, Hester was glad to note his seriousness. He had a bad habit of making clumsy jokes concerning the hermit's crazy feelings about her. In fact, more than once she'd bitterly regretted ever telling Rob about the old man's fancied link between her and the brand mark on his cheek. . . .

She could have been no older than four when, seeing

the outcast on the street one morning, she had trotted up and said, "Pray, Mr. Eben, sir, doth that *H* stand for my name—Hester?" She had just learned how to spell it.

She would always remember how he'd recoiled, clapping his hand to the branded cheek. In those days he was even more of an outcast, and very few people ever spoke to him at all.

And then the tears had come, running down the dirty old cheeks and over the scar itself, as he slowly removed his hand and said, "Why . . . why, yes, child. It doth. It doth indeed stand for *Hester.*"

And she had believed him, not then being able to *say* the word *heretic,* let alone understand it.

Her aunt had tried to explain as she angrily bustled her away. "He was branded thus for the terrible sin of heresy, you foolish girl! He believed his two babes should not be baptized until they had grown old enough to think for themselves."

Later, when Hester had gone on to question her, Aunt Elizabeth said, "And the branding was but a small part of his punishment. Less than six months later, the good Lord smote his house with the smallpox and carried away his wife and babes and all."

This had chilled Hester. "Was *my* father a heretic then, that the Lord should—?"

"Stop thy mouth, child! Thy father and mother were both God-fearing Presbyterians. The smallpox that took them was a natural calamity. And never again ask such impertinent questions of your elders. Even of such wretched Ishmaels as Eben Cranshaw!"

Hester had heeded that warning, but whenever Eben saw her from that day on, his haggard face would light up and he'd say, "Ah, Hester, my sweetheart! Come kiss thy mark upon my cheek!"—sending her running away in terror.

Rob could imitate that with horrible accuracy. But he'd only done it once. Coming from *him*, it hadn't been so frightening, yet it had seemed twenty times more embarrassing.

"How dare you!" she had said, slapping him on the bloodroot *H* he'd daubed on his own cheek.

"I was only aping Crazy Eben!" he'd protested.

"Well—well *don't!*" she had gasped. "Don't you ever do it again! Ever! . . ." Then, relenting a little: "It has become one of my nightmares. And your imitation be too realistic!"

He had apologized, and they never spoke of it again. But—

"Ha!" Rob's cry startled her out of her reverie. "Methinks we have found it! The scene of the evil deed!"

They had reached the very edge of the ruin. He was pointing to the chimney corner, to the old fireplace with its blackened stones and crumbling mortar and cracked hearthstone. The ashes and charred remnants of a fire there could only have been made very recently.

Everything else seemed to have been accumulating on the uneven floor for years: the rubble of rocks and pebbles; the bare patches of earth—some of it red, some of it black with powdered charcoal that had once been floorboards; the clumps of weeds, tall and brown; and flatter patches of vegetation, some still green. There were mossy patches, too, on what was left of a great oak beam that lay between them and the fireplace, as well as sinister fleshy crops of fungus, white and corpselike.

Stepping over the beam, Rob said, "Stay behind me. There are footprints in these damp patches. . . . Many . . . Same person . . . We may learn much from them if we take care not to destroy them."

There didn't appear to be that many to Hester. And those she could see were very confused, faint, and incomplete where the rubble took over from the damp dirt.

But Rob seemed to be using a different kind of vision altogether. "Walks with splayed feet . . . ," he murmured as he advanced inch by inch. "Somewhat ungainly . . . rolling gait."

"How do you know *that*?" she asked.

"Heels, see," he said, crouching in front of a particularly clear pair of prints. "Fainter at the outer edges. Worn down."

No, he wasn't joking, she decided. Not even when he gave a loud whoop and, still crouching, leaped the next few feet to the fireplace.

"And here!" he said. "Right in front of the hearth! What I was looking for yesterday in back of Goody Willson's. No heels at all, but the toes digging deeper where he stooped to the fire."

But she wasn't looking. *She* was stooping now.

"What's this?" she said, picking up something just to the side of him. "Another burr?"

He turned his head, frowning. "Yes," he said. Then: "Don't touch!"

To her surprise, he was pouncing on something she hadn't even seen, near where the burr had been. It was a small, wrinkled, brownish leaf.

"Burdock," he said, picking it up carefully by its stalk. "From the same herb. But . . ." He was twisting the stalk, turning the leaf over and back again. "This is a young leaf, yet old."

"What do you mean?" she said.

"I mean it fell from the plant many months ago. It is smooth now, with the wetness. Otherwise it would have been somewhat shriveled."

"Is it important?"

"It could be a very important sign. Look around. There has been no burdock plant growing in *here*. And I know of none that grows nearby neither."

"Could it have been blown here?"

He shook his head. "I doubt it. Besides, the burrs do not blow around. They get *carried* around. On fur or cloth."

"Could it have been stuck to the mud on someone's shoes, then?"

"Nay!" he said. "See how clean it be. No traces of mud." He frowned. "'Tis a sign, sure enough. If only we could riddle its meaning."

He put it carefully into his fringed bag.

"But *this* takes no riddling!" said Hester.

There was a rusty iron ring, still embedded in the mortar between two of the stones at the side of the fireplace. It had probably once been used for hooking ladles onto. But lately it had been put to a much more sinister purpose. Hester was pointing to the scrap of twine still fastened to it.

Rob took out his knife and cut the knot. "Aye," he said, examining it. "The same kind." He put that in his bag, too. "'Tis where the cat must have been tethered. . . . But have a care." He was now staring at a large stone that was lying on the hearth in front of the fireplace. It was crudely shaped, with straight edges. Clumps of rough, dry mortar were still clinging to its sides. "This seems to have fallen recently." He looked up at the battered chimney stack and one of the gaps that had appeared in it near the top. "Luckily there is no high wind today," he said. "But you must stand well back even so."

Hester moved back a couple of paces, but Rob himself stayed where he was, turning the stone over in his hands.

"Huh!" he grunted, holding it still and frowning at one of the rough corners.

"What is it?"

"Blood."

Forgetting his warning about falling masonry, Hester moved closer and peered at the stone. All she could see was a small, brownish stain. It was so small that she would probably not have seen it if he hadn't pointed it out.

"Blood?" she asked.

"Aye. Dried." He spit on a finger and rubbed it gingerly on the stain. "*Someone* wasn't careful enough!" he murmured.

She stared at his wet finger. The part of the stain transferred there did have a slightly redder, pinker look.

"Some*one*—or some*thing*?" she said, thinking of the cat that had been tethered nearby.

His frown had been very fierce. Then it lightened as he shrugged. "Who knows?" he said, putting the stone down and peering once more at the rubble underfoot. Then something else caught his eye, and he pounced on one of the small heaps of pebbles and rocks.

To her it looked like a tuft of tangled roots, just peeping out from under, but as he tugged it clear she saw it was something quite different.

"Huh!" he grunted again, staring down at the scrap of braided yarn, about three inches long, that now lay on the palm of his hand.

It was damp and dirty and faded, but as Hester looked closer she saw that it was made of three different-colored strands: yellow, red, and (she guessed) white.

"A piece of someone's sash or belt?" she murmured. "A woman's or girl's?"

She shuddered slightly, thinking of the Morton females and wondering if it, too, might be bloodstained. It wasn't *that* old though, surely, she thought.

"I don't know," he said, looking as puzzled as she felt. "It might not have had anything to do with the cat or the person who brought it. It was not left here recently, that is for sure. Even so . . ." He put it into the fringed bag.

"But speaking of the cat and—and the person—do you have a picture now of . . . of what took place?" Hester asked, half dreading the answer.

Rob shook his head, frowning darkly again. "No clear one. Not yet. Only of a very restless, sudden person. I can tell that by his footprints. Maybe he'd simply come in here out of curiosity, or for shelter from the storm on

Thursday morning. Without the branding iron or even the makings of a fire. Maybe after the idea had come he had to leave the cat securely trussed while he went to fetch those things."

Hester scowled. "He must be a madman!"

"Aye ... well ..."

Still frowning, Rob continued his search, inch by inch, grunting, peering closer at first one object then another, shaking his head, moving on. And he'd just straightened up and was saying, "I think we have found all the signs that be of any use," when someone coughed, and they turned to see Crazy Eben standing by the fallen beam.

"The only signs that be of any use to men come from on high," he said. "Not from the dust."

Startled, Hester thought about Rob's recent words: "A restless, sudden person."

"For thee, lass," the old man said softly, placing something on the beam.

Rob seized the chance of questioning him. "Sir, did you see anyone in here on Thursday morning?"

"Eh?"

"In here. Did you see anyone?"

The hermit looked uneasy. "Only the ghosts come here," he said. "John Morton, his shade, sometimes. Jane Morton's, often. They come from beyond the flames. They come seeking ..." His voice had sunk to a whisper, faltering into silence.

"Seeking what, sir?"

The old man glared at Rob. "Their children, of course!" he said hoarsely. "The children whose scalps were took before their very eyes!" Then he calmed down, lowered his head, and murmured, "But only one of they, the half-wit boy, Young-John, ever comes, and only when neither father or mother be here."

Hester glanced at Rob and shook her head, but Rob pressed on.

"Sir—about Thursday *afternoon* now. Did you see anyone outside the meetinghouse? During the lecture?"

A faraway look had crept into the faded blue eyes.

"Aye," the old man said at last. He seemed to be searching for something an immense distance away. "The shade of Young-John Morton springeth up everywhere, nowadays. 'Tis another sign of the great fire to come. He be God's messenger, mark my words!"

Hester glanced at Rob again. The outcast was obviously rambling. Old Eben seemed to notice this movement and understand her thoughts. He sighed, touched the object on the beam, and said, "For thee, lass. Hester. Had she been spared, that would a been *her* name."

Then he turned and strode off without saying another word.

Hester stood stock-still, stunned, shaken.

"*Whose* name?" said Rob. "One of the Morton children?"

"No. I—" She bit her lip. "I—I think he was referring to his own baby daughter, who didn't live to be baptized. I never knew before that that would have been her— Oh, dear!"

Through tears, she looked down at the object that Rob had picked up from the beam and passed to her.

It was a small birch-bark cone, filled to the brim with

white candy. White maple sugar was very rare, and only Eben knew for sure which tree its syrup came from. He was as famous for it as Goody Pierce was for her candied violets. Every year, since Hester's first meeting with him, he'd left such a gift on her doorstep—sometimes in a cone like this, sometimes in the upper half of a goose's bill—and every year, in her growing horror of him, she had screamed and refused even to touch it.

Now she put it carefully into her apron pocket.

"Thank you, Mr. Cranshaw!" she called out into the mist that had swallowed him up. "Thank you very, very much!"

Rob was watching her face. "I see *you* don't picture him anymore," he said softly.

"What? As the kitten's tormentor?"

"Aye."

She shook her head. "No. Not really. You can never tell with— But no."

"Good," he said. "Then you will no longer be wasting time looking for deer tracks when hunting a wolf. And right now we must set our minds to finding the branding iron. It could be lying around somewhere within a few yards of this very ruin."

11

Investigators' Moon?

They spent most of the rest of that Saturday searching for the branding iron. They went through the long grass outside the ruin four or five times, beating it with sticks, before Rob was satisfied. Then they searched the weeds at the edges of the farm track down to the village. Both sides. Twice.

But without luck.

The only ray of hope came later in the afternoon, when they looked in on the cat and found it curled up fast asleep after its first good meal.

"Two saucers—two—of fish!" Nell announced proudly. "I *said* I'd have her eating by Sunday!"

But Mistress Brown had gloomier news.

"The witch-hunting lust is getting worse," she said. "Tell them what you have heard in the village, Nell."

Then the servant's face darkened. "Aye, well . . . ," she began.

It seemed that Goody Carter, the blacksmith's wife—almost as frail as Mistress Brown herself—had been mentioned.

"She was seen by her own granddaughter and some other little wenches. They said she was talking to a robin as she threw crumbs out for the birds—"

"Which she always does," said Mistress Brown. "As do many others, too. Including thee, Nell."

"Aye," said Nell, "but this time—they *said*—the clouds above parted and the red on the fowl's breast turned the color of lavender."

"Pshaw! A trick of the light!" said Mistress Brown.

Nell shrugged and went on to tell of another report. This was about the sighting of a skunk circling the house of the widow Evans. "Three times, widdershins, in broad daylight. And pausing to shake its front paw in anger at those espying it."

"Nonsense!" said Hester. "Skunks do not behave so!"

"Had it shaken its *tail* at them, I might a believed it," said Rob.

"But that is why they say it must have been the devil in the shape of a skunk," said Mistress Brown. "Come a-visiting Widow Evans."

She continued to look very disturbed, even when they told her of the success of their investigations so far.

"I wish you could prove *who* did this," she muttered.

"We are getting closer, I'm sure," said Hester.

Nell had made up *her* mind the moment they'd spoken of Eben's visit to the ruin.

"*Who*, mistress? That crazy old fool is who, I'll wager on't! He done it to try to make us all believe he really do get messages from God."

"Nay!" said Mistress Brown. "Eben would not treat a poor dumb creature so in *that* cause."

"I do not believe he would do it in *any* cause," said Hester. "Not now."

"No," said Mistress Brown. "Whoever it was, did it to make people believe that poor Goody Willson was receiving messages from the *devil.*"

"And I am certain sure Eben didn't do it," said Rob.

"How so?" said Nell, glaring at him as if to say she'd be contradicted by her mistress and even Hester, but not by *him.*

"Because those were not his footprints in there," said Rob. "When not dressed up to come into town, he wears moccasins, like me. And his feet are much bigger than those that made the prints."

Later, in the woodshed, Rob mentioned Eben again. Hester had already added to the list of signs the footprints, the rusty ring with its scrap of twine, and most of the other items, when he said, "There is also what Eben told us."

"What about?" she asked, with the quill pen poised.

"Seeing the ghost on Thursday afternoon."

"Ghost?" She almost flung the pen down. "He is always seeing ghosts. We cannot record *that* as a sign!"

"But he could have caught a glimpse of a living being and *thought* it a ghost."

She picked up the pen and stroked her nose thoughtfully. "Well," she murmured, "we already know that it *must* have been a living being that placed the cat there. So why mar the record with ghosts?"

"But—"

"I will *not* have ghosts! With this book—with our investigations—we are trying to *fight* superstition. Not encourage it."

"All right, all right! Content! There is no need to get angry!"

"Who is getting—?" She checked herself. "I'm sorry. It has been a very tiring day."

"Yes," he said, suddenly sympathetic. "We must get a good night's sleep, and tomorrow we will resume our search."

"Well . . ." She hesitated. "'Tis the Sabbath tomorrow, and Aunt Elizabeth is very strict about keeping it holy."

"What be that?" he said. "All I am suggesting is that after meeting we go for a walk to discuss the sermon. Even she will approve of *that.*"

"But that would be lying!"

"Oh, no, 'twould not!" he replied. "Mr. Phipps is sure to talk about the growing signs of witchcraft in the village. And what will we be doing but seeking to disprove the most striking of those signs?"

She found herself smiling. "Sometimes you really do begin to sound like a Boston lawyer!" she said.

"Aye, well," he murmured. "If this be an ensample of the kind of chase the law requires of its chiefs, maybe I will make my grandfather happy after all!"

"Then you'd better work harder at your letters, after this matter has been resolved," she retorted.

"Huh!" was all he replied to that.

But for a time this exchange had made her feel better. Whatever the result of their investigations, at least *some* good seemed to be coming out of them.

Then gradually her mind returned to the matter itself. *Would* it be resolved? And—what was more important—could it be resolved before innocent people lost their lives?

That night, in the gently wavering candlelight, she sat up in bed with a shawl around her shoulders and her book propped on her knees. She was studying the latest notes, under the heading *Found in the Morton homestead ruinnes.* The first of the new signs listed was *The remaines of a fyre, made recently and large enough for the heating of the branding iron.*

The footprints came next. And to this they had been able to add the actual size: *almost 9 inches long and 3½ inches wide at broadest part.* This was because Rob had used the twine from the ring and tied two new knots in it, one to measure the length of the clearest print, and one the width. They were then able to check these against a measuring rod when they got back.

Hester looked up and gazed at the window. The edge of the moon was just beginning to peep through one of the panes. . . .

The knots had been Rob's idea; the final *accurate* measuring, hers. Neither would have been much good for this record without the other.

She thought so, anyway.

She turned back to the list. *The heeles badly worn at the outer edges.*

Well, that was all very fine. "But we cannot go around asking people to lift their feet for our inspection," she had objected.

"We can if other signs point to just one person," was Rob's reply to that.

Her aunt's snores suddenly soared louder from the

next room. Tomorrow she'd be complaining of a sore throat. Then, Sabbath or not, she'd be pleading with Rob to bring her herbs to soothe it.

Ah, well . . .

Twine fastened to ring in fyreplace was the next entry. *Same kind as found on the cat. Doubtless used to tether it.*

Then came *Small burdock leaf & burr from same herbe.* Here she could only think of adding, *How did they get there where no such plantes grow?*

Neither of them could give a satisfactory answer to that. Not for the leaf, anyway.

Suddenly, she frowned at the riot of patterns on the patchwork quilt. What was it that had just crossed her mind so rapidly—too rapidly even to identify? Something to do with burdock . . .

Burdock. Burdock . . .

No, it wouldn't come.

She went on with her checking.

Large, loose stone on hearth, probably fallen from chimney stacke. Small bludde stayne in one corner. Cat's? Or personne's?

Earlier, in the woodshed, Rob had declared that it was probably the cat's blood after all, and that the creature could have been tethered to the fireplace when the stone fell.

"It *could* have caused the wound on the head. Striking it a glancing blow there, and maybe on the leg also."

"*Could? Maybe?*" she said. "It does not seem a very clear picture this time."

"No," was all he replied to that, his frown darkening.

So all she had added to the entry was, *Probably the cat's own bludde,* leaving it at that.

After the entry for the scrap of braided yarn, she found it impossible to add even a *probably.* Just: *Scrappe of braided yarn. Red, yellow, and white. 2½ inches long.*

Nevertheless, it was the same as with the burdock leaf. She just couldn't help feeling that it was somehow very important, that she had seen it before somewhere.

And she went over it one more time, trying to picture who she'd seen wearing it as a belt or sash, and when.

But nothing took shape in her mind except a long and lengthening red-and-white-and-yellow belt that went snaking in and out and around the waists of all the girls and women in the village, fitting none of them . . . and only ending . . . in a great . . . tangled . . . ball. . . .

Her head jerked, rousing her from the doze she'd been dropping into.

That had been her last entry. After it had come her fight with Rob over whether or not to enter Eben's ghosts.

The moon was now showing a larger portion of itself at the window. She tried to remember the name the Indians gave this one. It wasn't the Hunters' Moon, she knew. That came in the fall.

She shrugged. Maybe they should call it the Investigators' Moon and hope it would continue to be helpful to them. *More* helpful, in fact—because so far the signs had only proved *where* the deed had been done, not who had done it.

Hester sighed. If only they could find that branding iron . . . if only . . .

She blinked. She must have been nodding off again. She looked at the window. The moon seemed to be in the same place.

Then, as she stared, her eyes began to trace out the initial letter of her name among the twelve small squares of glass, where the frames stood out dark against the moon's silver. *H*—yes. One at the top in the center, one at the bottom.

It was an old habit of hers. An old habit, but a new regret. Ever since she'd gone hunting with Rob for the letters of the alphabet in natural objects, she'd been irked by the fact that there seemed to be no *H*'s.

The curvy letters were the easiest. *O*'s abounded. In the eyes of certain birds. In daisy-headed flowers. Even in the spinning ripples made by heavy raindrops on the surfaces of ponds and puddles. Some were beautiful, like the gold wedding rings, as she thought of them, in the centers of the fluffy, pearly blooms of one of the everlasting flowers. There were similar golden *O*'s on the wings of some butterflies, too, and—oh, everywhere, in creatures and plants of all kinds.

Yet no *H*. Not in all nature. Except where it had been branded on living flesh.

Of course, it stood to reason that the letters made out of straight rigid lines *would* be more difficult to find in natural objects. Even so, the sloping and slanting ones were really quite plentiful if you looked carefully. *V*'s and *Y*'s, for instance—in the veins of leaves, or rabbits' pricked-up ears, or the flight formations of geese and ducks. Once your eyes were attuned to the task, *W*'s could be picked out from the long grasses and reeds and cattails almost anytime.

But *H*'s and *T*'s and *E*'s—no.

Though even the last two could be found with less difficulty than *H*'s, if you were prepared to do a little adjusting, a little mutilating. They had once formed two ragged, spiny *E*'s by tearing a pin oak leaf in half, down the middle. And there was the time when she'd had to stop Rob from doing something similar to a dragonfly.

She shuddered even now as she thought of it. . . .

They'd been sitting on a grassy slope at the side of the pond in Mistress Brown's garden when he'd caught one in his cupped hands. It was a beautiful creature with a slender, bright blue body and four gossamer wings. She thought at first he'd caught it just to show her.

But, alas, no.

To her horror, he said, "Look! When I remove the lower wings it will make a perfect *T.*"

She caught his hand before he could do any such thing. "No! How *could* you be so cruel?"

He blinked at her. He hadn't been long out of captivity then. "Cruel?"

"Yes. That is a living creature! It will cause it terrible pain!"

He thought a moment. "Very well," he said, "I will kill it first. *Then* it will feel no pain when I remove its wings."

She absolutely forbade it and made him let the dragonfly go.

He still looked very perplexed, and once again their friendship might have ended. But luckily there was a patch of small pale blue flowers in the grass nearby—the sort Nell called "blueys." They had four petals each.

"Here," she said, plucking one and removing a petal. *"There's a T."*

Sure enough, the small blue cross had been transformed. The remaining three petals did make a kind of rounded letter *T*. But it was nowhere near as sharply outlined as the amputated dragonfly would have been.

"Huh! . . . And doth not the *flower* feel pain?"

She couldn't help smiling at the memory. He'd caught her *there*! Even then he must have had something of the lawyer in him.

But she was glad to think that he'd never be prepared to do that to a dragonfly nowadays. Now he had far more sympathy for the suffering of living creatures. As with the cat. As with Eben and the horrible brand. She'd seen the way he'd looked at the old man's cheek, and—

Suddenly she sat bolt upright.

Of course!

Eben . . . the *H* for *heresy* . . . the dragonfly and the flower . . . the small blue cross that became a *T* . . . "*T* for your thief" . . . Mr. Carter . . . the irons gathering dust in the tavern . . .

With the pictures and words flying through her mind, she clambered out of bed. Making sure the candle was stuck firmly on the spike of the metal save-all, she went downstairs, pursued by the snores of her aunt.

Then, after throwing her cloak over her nightclothes and slipping her shoes on, she stole out of the house.

Two minutes later, she was back in bed, her heart thumping.

She turned to a blank page, and with Rob's red crayon, which she'd brought back from the shed, she made two quick strokes, paused, turned the book upside down, and made two more—this time more slowly and carefully. "There!" she murmured, with her "great" smile spreading all over her face. "I have found it, I have found it! Wait until I show Rob this!"

12
Rob Seizes the Evidence

The next morning, with the first silver glimmer in the sky, Hester quietly let herself out of the house, hoping that her aunt would sleep for another half hour at least. It was a risk that had to be taken. It was imperative that Rob should learn of her find at the earliest possible moment. There would be urgent work for him to do later, and it must be well planned.

Under the trees it seemed almost to be night again. But the trail was wide enough not to slow her down much. Only when she veered away from it, just before reaching the MacGregor clearing, and took the path into the forest did it become more difficult. But by then the sky was already getting lighter. And in her excitement she felt she could have floated over the tree roots and any fallen limbs like one of the very witches she scorned to believe in.

A heavy splash told her she was close to her destination, and—yes, sure enough—there on a log at the edge of the forest pool was draped a white towel, next to a darker bundle of cloth.

This, she knew, was where Rob bathed every morning at dawn, even in winter, except when the ice was too thick. It was another Indian habit that he swore nothing would ever break him of. "'Tis bad enough sleeping under a roof in an airless box all night!" he still sometimes grumbled.

She was now close enough to see the colors of the tartan blanket next to the towel—but where was *he*? There were slow-spreading ripples on the surface of the dark water, but the floating matted patches of old leaves seemed undisturbed. Was he playing one of his stupid pranks?

She clucked with impatience and called out, "Rob! Where are you? Come show yourself. *Now!* This is most urgent!"

Suddenly, one of the leaf islands erupted and his head and shoulders broke the surface. Judging from the surprise on his face, he must not have heard her voice.

"What—what are you doing *here*?" he gasped.

"Come out and I will show you. I have found it! Hurry!"

"Turn thy back, then," he said, swimming toward the log.

Blushing, she heard him clamber to the bank. He could scarce have dried himself properly before he came to her side, saying, "*What* have you found?"

He really did look like some strange Indian-Scottish chief in that early light, bundled up in the blanket, with his hair all spiky and dripping.

"This," she said, taking the record book from under her cloak.

He frowned. "But I didn't know you had lost it."

"Not the book! *This!*"

She withdrew a loose page. It was already neatly

folded in half. Just under the fold, with the letter's cross-bar actually on the crease, she had drawn a careful capital *T* in red crayon.

"'Tis an odd time for a lesson," he murmured.

"Never mind the time, dunce! What is the letter?"

He bridled. "Why, *what* dunce? *T,* of course! *T* for *tomahawk!*"

"Good," she said. "Now let me see you make a *T* just like it. Here." She turned the folded paper over to its blank half. "With the crossbar along the fold, starting here"—she indicated a red spot—"and ending here, at this other small mark.... And start the middle stem *there,* and end it *here.*"

With the paper resting on the book, she held it steady. Still looking puzzled, he took the crayon and did what she asked.

"There," he said. "Another *T.* So what is—?"

"Yes!" She snatched up the folded sheet. "Another *T* for *thief.* And see now what *that* gives us!"

He stared at the fully opened sheet, at her *T* and his *T,* which together now formed—

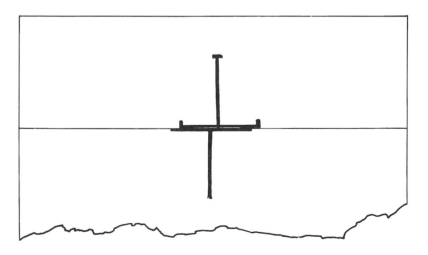

"A cross! Like unto *the* cross!"

"Aye," she said. "The cross with which the cat was branded. And now we know where that instrument be!"

"We—in—you mean—?"

"Where you have seen it but two days ago. Yes. Hanging in the chimney corner of the tavern."

He growled. "To think I might a grasped it in my hands!"

"Do not fret. You *will* be grasping it, before long!" she said.

"Oh?"

"Yes. That is why I have come this early. So that when the tavern be emptied, with everyone eager to hear Mr. Phipps's sermon, thirsting for any further news of the Massachusetts witches, you will be in there seizing that *T* iron. I have no doubt but that it will match the cat's brand. It will be final proof positive."

"Just so!" he said, eager eyed himself now. "I will make some excuse on the way to meeting and hold back until the way be clear."

"Good!" she said. "As an *investigator* thou'rt certainly no dunce. But now I must fly."

Hester would remember all her life the moment Rob slipped into the meetinghouse later that morning. They were singing the Fortieth Psalm and she had stolen yet another glance back at the door, prompted by the words:

> With expectation for the Lord
> I wayted patiently,

And hee inclined unto mee,
Also he heard my cry.

And that was precisely when Rob walked in and quietly took his place in the back row!

As the singing droned on, she tried to read his expression.

He brought mee out of dreadful-pit,
Out of the miery clay;
And set my feet upon a rock,
Hee stablished my way.

His features were impassive as usual. *Indian* impassive, she thought with a flash of impatience.

And in my mouth put a new song,
Of prayse—

A sharp dig in the ribs startled her.

"Stop thy staring around, Hester!" hissed Aunt Elizabeth.

But Hester was content at last. Her heart was beating joyfully. For Rob's eyes had met hers, and for the briefest instant he had nodded *yes*!

She joined in the singing as lustily as any of them now.

Blest is the man that on the Lord
Maketh his trust abide;
Nor doth the proud respect, nor such
To lies as turne aside. . . .

Now we will see, she was thinking, what those who turn aside to lies make of the truth when confronted with this new evidence.

13
Rob's Two Questions

"So there it is," said Hester, that afternoon in Mistress Brown's parlor.

"The instrument that made the mark upon the cat and nearly had its mistress hung."

The branding iron was lying on the table, next to her record book. That was open at the page where Rob had not long before made a new drawing.

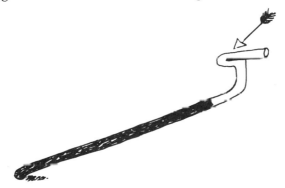

It was very accurate and showed plainly that the instrument had been wrought from a single thin cylindrical bar of iron, bent at the top in the shape of an upright

T. It showed also that the bar was black except at the top. "That is where the blackening has been burned off," Rob had said while drawing. "All the other irons are black through their whole lengths. 'Tis the only one that has been used lately."

Then he'd pricked with the point of his knife at the part of the branding iron where the bar had been bent back on itself to cross the *T.* "There!" he said, scraping out of the loop a black, sticky fragment. "A piece of scorched fur."

Which was when he'd drawn the triumphant arrow.

Now Mistress Brown and Nell were staring at that particular spot.

"And you believe 'twas Peacemaker Cleary?" said Mistress Brown.

"There is no doubt in *my* mind," said Rob.

"Mine either," said Hester. "I *had* wondered, thinking it be too clever for him. But then Rob reminded me that Peacemaker was the only village boy with wit enough to be his rival at identifying and gathering herbs."

"But careless and slovenly," said Rob. "Getting his roots mixed up. Plucking leaves at the wrong times. And I'll warrant *he* never cleans out that sack of his. Which is what has also helped betray him."

"How so?" said Mistress Brown.

"The burrs," said Rob. "And the burdock leaf. They had probably lurked in his sack for months. As also did this." He held up the white hair.

"Which has explained the presence of *this* in the Morton ruins," said Hester, her eyes shining with triumph as she picked up the scrap of braid for the women's inspection.

"What is it?" asked Mistress Brown, peering closer. "And what doth it have to do with that—*hair*, is it?"

"The hair is that of a dog," said Rob. "The Phipps's dog Captain."

"And this braid is part of a ball," said Hester. "Made by Mistress Phipps from a bundle of scraps, for the children to play with."

"Aye!" said Nell. "I remember it now. A waste of good material, I thought! But—"

"That ball was used by them to entertain the dog," said Rob. "When it was a pup."

"Before it was lost!" said Hester. Her eyes were still sparkling. It was only an hour ago that she had finally remembered where she had seen the braid before.

Mistress Brown looked faintly bewildered. "Lost?" she said. "The ball?"

"Or the pup?" said Nell, looking equally puzzled.

"Both," said Rob. "They were missed at the same time, last summer."

"Some thought the ball had fallen down the well," said Hester. "And that the pup had gone seeking it and itself had fallen in and was drowned."

"But happily the pup was found alive, two days later," said Rob.

"Ah, yes!" exclaimed Nell. "By Peacemaker Cleary! He claimed he had found it beside South Creek Swamp. Whither it had strayed."

"Aye!" growled Rob. "For which he was rewarded by Mr. Phipps with a whole shilling!"

"But now we know 'twas not so," said Hester. "Now we know *he* had 'ticed away the pup, by tempting it with its own ball."

"And then had captured it," said Rob. "Thrusting both ball and pup into his sack and carrying them off privily to a hiding place."

"The Morton ruins?" said Mistress Brown.

"Aye!" said Rob. "And that is how a hair from the pup came to be left inside the sack."

"And when he used that same sack for transporting the cat," Hester continued, "these things must have clung to its fur. The pup's hair, the burrs, the violet petal—*and the burdock leaf.*"

Her eyes were glowing again. That leaf had proved to be the first key. And she'd been the one who spotted that connection, too, earlier that afternoon. That was when she finally remembered how Rob had once collected burdock leaves to soothe one of Aunt Elizabeth's sore throats, and that Peacemaker had also collected these, for other people.

"So," said Mistress Brown, nodding with satisfaction. "The wretch's slovenliness hath been his undoing."

"Yes," said Hester. "But sloven though he is, I guess he would be clever enough to form a cross out of two *T*'s."

"I am *sure* of it!" said Mistress Brown. "I have heard Mr. Williams say it more than once—how Peacemaker Cleary could be almost as clever as thee, child, if only he would put his neck into his work."

Hester wasn't sure about *that.* She was very proud of her standing as a scholar fit to teach others.

But now Nell was giving *her* opinion. "That one be very sly and cunning. And an arch at lying. He will wriggle his way out of this—mark my words. He'll deny everything."

"We'll see," said Mistress Brown. "Luke Lawson is no fool. The Reverend Phipps neither. . . . But 'tis no use presenting them with your report on the Sabbath. I'll arrange for you to see them both tomorrow morning."

"Good," said Rob. "It will give me time to seek the answers to two questions. To complete my picture."

Rob then went on to describe how it was now shaping in his hunter's imagination. How he saw the cat being scooped up and put in the sack on Thursday morning, probably on the path behind Goody Willson's house. How it had been carried to the Morton ruins. How Cleary had probably been hoping to be rewarded with another shilling for "finding" the animal, after keeping it there a few days and causing its owner great distress.

"But then the thunderstorm started," Rob continued. His eyes darkened as he narrowed them against the dazzle of a shaft of sunlight that had suddenly come beaming down from the window. He took a step back. "And the thunderstorm destroyed his wicked plan."

"How so?" whispered Mistress Brown.

"A merciful act of God!" murmured Nell.

Rob shook his head. "There was no *mercy* in it. It only caused him to think of an even more wicked plan."

"Oh, and what was that, pray?" asked Mistress Brown, looking up at him.

"One of the thunderclaps shook the ruins so fiercely that a heavy stone was loosed from the chimney stack and fell—"

"Giving the cat a blow on the head in passing," said Hester.

"A glancing blow, fortunately," said Rob. "Rendering the animal senseless without killing it instantly. The same stone probably struck its rear right leg also." Still frowning darkly, Rob flashed a defiant glance at Hester. "Alas that it did not fall on *Cleary's* head!" he growled.

"You ought not to say 'alas' for that, Rob!" Hester flashed back at him. "I keep telling you—"

"Hush, child!" said Mistress Brown. She turned to Rob. "You have not yet told us of the wretch's other plan."

"No, ma'am," said Rob. "But when he had recovered from his own cowardly fright at the fall, he saw the cat lying there stiff and still and thought it dead. He, too, must have believed it an act of God, sent to thwart his plan. But then, with his quick weasel's cunning—"

"The cunning of the devil!" Nell cut in. "Sorry, lad— go on with thy picture. I think I see its shaping anew."

Rob nodded. "Then he saw his way to putting it to his own evil use after all. The act of God that had prevented him from squeezing money from Goody Willson could be made to cost her more than a shilling or two."

"It could be made to cost her her very *life*!" added Hester.

"By proving her to be a witch—ayc!" said Mistress Brown. "A witch whose familiar had been stricken down by a thunderbolt from God!"

"Just so, ma'am," said Rob. "And seeing the fireplace so close to the seemingly dead cat minded him how it could be done. By singeing the cat's fur with a hot iron to simulate a lightning strike."

"Yes!" said Hester. "And as he hurried back to the village to fetch the makings of the fire, his cunning brain suggested the shape of a cross to make it seem even *more* an act of God's vengeance!"

Then Rob completed his picture by telling them how he imagined Cleary branding the unconscious creature.

"A deed done hurriedly, in his impatience to carry out his plan. So that he did not wait to get the iron hot enough to do more than scorch the fur."

"Thank goodness!" murmured Hester.

"But I'll warrant that he was pleased with the result even so," said Rob. "Thinking that the cunning black cross on the creature's flank would be sure to have Goody Willson cried out for a witch."

Rob concluded by picturing Cleary carrying the branded creature back to the village in his sack, then waiting for the lecture to start before depositing the cat where everyone would see it on their way out.

The account was punctuated by many a growl from Nell, but her mistress listened in thoughtful silence.

"Yes . . .," Mistress Brown murmured when Rob was through. "But it doth not tell us *why* he wished to see poor Goody Willson hang."

Nell snorted. "Huh! Just out of spite and malice and sheer wickedness! Which he will deny. He will deny it all. Stealing the creature, branding it, everything."

"You think so?" Hester asked, uneasy all at once.

"Aye," said Nell. "Of *course* he will!"

"But his footprints—"

"Even if they are his," Mistress Brown began, "which I do not doubt—"

"We will soon prove it," said Rob.

"Even *though* they are his," Mistress Brown went on, "he'll say he made them later, when he just happened to wander innocently into that place. After the deed was done already by someone else."

"Aye!" said Nell. "Just so!"

Hester was feeling quite chilled by now. "Then what about this branding iron from his father's tavern?" she protested. "How can he explain *that*?"

"Why, child!" said the old lady. "He'll simply say that *anyone* could have gone in and taken it, the tavern door being so seldom locked."

"And the burrs and the burdock leaf, the hair and the petal?" Hester said defiantly, giving her hair a toss.

"Tush!" said Nell. " 'They fell from *Rob's* bag.' That's what he'll say. . . . He'll even turn it as proof that *Rob* did the whole deed. A savage Indian trick."

"*Ridiculous!*" Hester exploded.

"Not ridiculous to Peacemaker Cleary," said Mistress Brown, with that trembly shake of the head. "And 'twill not sound all that ridiculous to the gentlemen, neither. After all, Rob did live with the Indians."

Hester's face was now burning with indignation. But Rob's was as impassive as ever.

"You speak the truth, Mistress Brown," he said. "Which is why I need to have my questions answered."

"Aye?" said the old lady. "So what are they?"

"Well, the first you may be able to answer yourselves," he said. "The second is one that only Goody Willson can answer."

"I'll be taking her a basket of dainties this afternoon," said Nell. "I will ask her then, if you'll tell me what it is."

"But first, young man, your question to us?" asked Mistress Brown.

"It is this," said Rob. "Do you remember the Morton family and, in particular, the son, Young-John?"

"Ah, the half-wit," said Nell. "I remember him very clear, poor lad!"

"I, too," said Mistress Brown sadly. "Is *that* your question?"

"Only partly," said Rob. "What I really need to know is what he looked like. Around the time of his death."

Hester was now staring at him curiously, but he avoided her eyes.

"Well, let's see," said Mistress Brown. "Young-John Morton. . . . He'd a been about eleven or twelve. A sickly, skinny boy."

"A squirmy, squirrelly lad," Nell chimed in. "Never still. Allus prying and peering, with a knowing leer on his face that made you think sometimes he wasn't as daft as he made out to be. A—" She suddenly paused. Then: "Why!" she gasped. "Not unlike Peacemaker Cleary, now I come to think!"

Mistress Brown was smiling. "And why shouldn't there be a likeness? Though I must confess *I* don't quite remember it."

"You never seen him as oft as I, ma'am," Nell said stiffly.

"Peace, Nell!" said Mistress Brown. "As I was about to say: Why shouldn't there be some resemblance betwixt Young-John Morton and Peacemaker Cleary? After all, Young-John's mother was Ezra Cleary's aunt."

"*I* was coming to that!" muttered Nell.

"Does that answer thy question, Rob?" asked Mistress Brown.

"Yes," he said. "I will have to think on it more—but yes."

Hester was still staring at him curiously.

"And thy second question?" said Mistress Brown. "For Goody Willson?"

"Aye," said Rob. "I need to know if she'd had harsh words with Peacemaker recently. Perhaps on Wednesday. Or even Thursday morning itself."

"To see if he bore her a grudge," said Hester.

"Huh!" grunted Nell. "Who *doesn't* that one bear a grudge against? But I will ask her, if it helps."

"Yes, it will help," said Rob. "It—"

"It will help to stablish a motive for this evil deed," said Hester haughtily, giving Rob a sharp look.

He had already discussed this second question with her, and she'd approved. But the first question had taken her completely by surprise—and, as the investigatrix in charge of the cause, she strongly disapproved of being kept in the dark by her assistant.

14
The Secret Witness

The scene in the meetinghouse vestry at ten o'clock the next morning was very similar to the one in Mistress Brown's parlor. Once again, the branding iron and Hester's record book were lying on the table. This time, though, all the other items of evidence were set out also: the pieces of twine, the burrs, the leaf, the dog hair, the scrap of braided yarn, even the violet petal and the grains of red earth.

And this time Hester and Rob went through the whole story of their investigation without interruption. Mr. Lawson and the Reverend Phipps sat there listening intently, grave faced, silent except for an angry indrawn breath from Mr. Phipps when Rob explained the significance of the braided yarn and the spaniel's hair.

"And we have heard only last evening," said Hester, winding up, "one further item of proof."

"Oh?" said Mr. Lawson. "And what may that be, pray?"

"It is that on Thursday morning, Goody Willson did catch Peacemaker Cleary in her yard attempting to steal her violets," said Hester. "And when she ordered him out, taking her broom to chase him away, he said, 'You wait, you old witch! I will make you pay for this!' "

The men's frowns deepened. Hester began to feel slightly uneasy. Surely, in the face of such proof, they couldn't be having any doubts?

"Also," said Rob, "we hope to bring a witness who saw him place the cat under the sycamore."

"Though it is not like to be necessary," said Hester, "with all this other evidence."

She was secretly *hoping* that it wouldn't be necessary to call that witness. As she'd told Rob earlier, "It might prove so unreliable as to blow up in our faces. Like the faulty blunderbuss that killed Mr. Evans when he tried to shoot the thieving fox."

But right now the men were speaking.

"This be a very grave matter," Mr. Lawson murmured.

"Very grave indeed," said Mr. Phipps. "And Peacemaker Cleary must be afforded the opportunity to give his own account."

Mr. Lawson nodded. "Of course. And that without further delay."

"Young man," said Mr. Phipps, turning to Rob, "will you be so kind as to step across to the tavern and ask him to see us here right away?"

"But do not tell him what for," Mr. Lawson quickly added. "Let him think it is merely some trifling matter."

Rob must have carried out this order perfectly. When he returned with Peacemaker Cleary, the boy seemed very unconcerned. Curious, but unconcerned.

His manner soon changed when he saw the branding iron.

White faced, he turned from one man to the other, twisting his hat in his hands. He even rolled his eyes toward the door, as if he were thinking of cutting and running. Then he took a tremendous grip on the hat.

"There hath been a very serious accusation made against thee, Peacemaker Cleary," said Mr. Lawson.

"'Tis a lie!" blurted Peacemaker. He rolled his eyes toward Hester and Rob this time. "A foul, wicked lie! They—"

"Silence!" roared Mr. Lawson. "You haven't even heard what it is yet!"

"The accusation," said Mr. Phipps, "is that you did steal and brand Goody Willson's cat yourself. Using this *T* iron to simulate a cross. What say you to that?"

Peacemaker was gaping.

"And have a care," growled Mr. Lawson, "how you answer. There be certain proofs that point the finger straight at *thee!*"

Then Peacemaker found his voice. "'Twas not my fault, sir! I was drove to't! 'Twas . . . 'twas the *devil* that drove me!"

"It usually is," said the minister dryly.

"No, sir! No!" Peacemaker protested. "I mean he was *inside* the cat, sir. Sent by the witch Gammer Willson."

"Go on," murmured Mr. Lawson, frowning.

"Yes, sir. 'Tis true, sir. She set it to trail me. It trailed me all the way from her house, it did. I had to throw rocks to make it avoid. To—to drive away the devil." He blinked at the minister. "As we are taught to do."

Hester could stand it no longer. "That is not true!" she said. "You carried it there in your herb sack. This burdock leaf proves it!"

"Be quiet, Hester," said Mr. Lawson. He turned to Peacemaker, who now had the beginnings of a triumphant leer quivering in his mouth corners. "And *did* you drive it away?"

The boy checked the leer, but there was still that confident glint in his eyes. "No, sir. It kept a-coming."

"All the way to the Morton place?" asked Mr. Phipps, looking rather surprised.

As well he might! thought Hester.

"I . . . uh . . ." Peacemaker didn't seem so sure now. "Morton place, sir?"

"Your footprint was found there!" Hester snapped.

Mr. Lawson frowned at her, but got to his feet and went around the table, making Peacemaker cringe as if he expected a buffeting.

"Stop cowering, boy!" said Mr. Lawson. "And lift up thy foot. Sole uppermost."

Blinking, Peacemaker obeyed. Mr. Lawson peered, then flipped open the record book.

"Now the other foot," he commanded. He looked at it and glanced at the footprint entry. "Hmm!" he murmured. "They correspond with the description given. What say you to that?"

But Peacemaker Cleary had been given too much time. "Well, yes, sir. Now you mention it, I *might* a been there. I do go there sometimes, to pray—"

"*What?*" snapped Mr. Phipps.

"To—to pray, sir!"

"To *pray*, boy?" said Mr. Phipps, looking outraged. "When the proper place for prayer, this house of God, is but a few paces across the street from you?"

"Well, yes, sir. But this was to pray for the destruction of the witches, sir. The Morton roons be where they sometimes meet, sir. To mix and boil their evil brews."

"And you attend such cabals?" said Mr. Lawson, looking shocked.

"Oh, no, sir, no! I just see signs of them. Like . . ." Peacemaker's eyes were roving around the table. "Yes, sir, like the burdock leaf *they* two found. That must a been part of the witches' stew. . . ." A look of indescribable cunning crept into his eyes. "Unless, sir, it dropped from that Indiand's own bag."

Hester was beginning to feel stomach-sick. This boy was an even worse and more wriggling liar than Nell had described.

"So you insist that the cat followed you that far, then?" Mr. Lawson said. "All the way to the Morton place?"

"A familiar haunt of yours," added Mr. Phipps, glancing at the braid. "Where you are wont to keep the animals you have stolen!"

Peacemaker Cleary gaped, shocked into silence for a moment.

It was Mr. Lawson who came to his rescue, unwittingly, by repeating his question.

"The Morton place, boy. You say the cat followed you all the way there? With you trying to drive it away with rocks?"

"Yes, sir. The devil be very persistent, sir."

"And did you not hit it in all that time?"

"Well . . . well, no, sir," said Peacemaker. "'Twas the big stone hit him. When we was in the roons. Just as he was going for my throat. Ready to rip my soul out, sir. Then the good Lord above struck him a blow that felled him. Yes, sir."

Even Rob's face was betraying indignation and revulsion now. But he kept silent.

"And then what?" said Mr. Phipps.

"I left the creature there for dead, sir."

"After you had branded it?" said Mr. Lawson quietly.

Peacemaker was ready for that.

"No, sir. I know nought about that. 'Twas the lightning struck it. God hisself, sir!"

"Have a care, boy!" the minister growled. "Be sure you do not take his name in vain!"

"Well—well, it *was* lightning struck the body, sir. Making a cross on't."

"So what next?" said Mr. Lawson.

"I fled, sir. Oh, but I was filled with terror—with holy terror, sir—I tell you, sir! I was in fear for my in-mortal soul!"

"And left the body in the ruins of the Morton place?" said Mr. Lawson.

"Yes, sir."

"Then how did it get here, outside the meeting-house?" said Mr. Phipps.

"I know not, sir," said Peacemaker. "Maybe it was transported here by God hisself—"

"You have been warned, boy!" said Mr. Phipps.

Peacemaker blinked and lowered his eyes. "Well, by

the devil then," he mumbled. "I—I know not. I was bewitched."

There was a short silence. Peacemaker wrung his hat. Mr. Phipps sighed. Hester glanced at Rob. Rob stared stonily out the window.

Then Mr. Lawson said, "Where were you during the lecture on Thursday, Peacemaker Cleary?"

Peacemaker looked up. "Why, in here, sir. In the meetinghouse. Listening to the minister tell of they witches up in Massachusetts."

"The whole time?" said Mr. Lawson.

"Yes, sir," said Peacemaker. "I would not a missed a word on't."

This time Rob did break in. Turning from the window, he said, "So how comes it that thou wast seen, Peacemaker Cleary? In the street. During the lecture."

Cleary jumped. "Eh? Me? 'Tis a lie! Seen by who? You? Her? You was both inside listening to the lecture yourselves. Eh? . . ."

Rob was shaking his head, the ghost of a smile on his lips. "No. Not by *us*. By someone who was definitely *not* within these walls." Rob turned to the men. "May we call him now, sirs? Just to look in from the doorway?"

Both men nodded.

As Rob crossed to the back door, Hester closed her eyes. It had taken almost an hour, earlier, to find Eben and get him to agree to come.

"And then it will only be to *look* in, Mr. Cranshaw," she had said. "And answer one simple question."

"Very well. For thee, my love," he'd said. "But I will

go no farther than the threshold, mind!"

"That will be far enough, sir," Rob had replied. "If you will just be on hand, outside."

Rob had wanted the old man to come with them right away. But Eben had insisted on following later, after he'd had time to change into what he called his town-visiting clothes. Then they'd had to leave him and hope he'd keep his word.

Now, when she heard the door open and Rob call out softly, "Mr. Cranshaw—we're ready, sir!" Hester sighed with relief and opened her eyes.

Eben was standing on the step, looking rather bewildered, scared, awed. The weather had turned chilly again, and a few lazy snowflakes were floating down onto his scorched and battered hat and frayed cloak.

Suddenly Peacemaker howled, "*That* old fool! What doth *he* know? What—?"

"Silence, boy!" roared Mr. Lawson.

Eben himself seemed unconscious of the outburst. His fearful, wondering eyes were ranging around the ceiling and walls. After all, Hester reminded herself, it was over thirty years since he'd been this close to entering the building.

Suddenly, Mr. Phipps's face softened. "Pray, come inside, Mr. Cranshaw," he said. "'Tis cold out there. And this is but the vestry, open to all for town business."

"Aye, come in, man!" said Mr. Lawson gruffly. "That draft from the open door is freezing my feet!"

Eben hesitated a moment longer. Then he took off his hat and slowly, cautiously, entered the room. He still seemed not to notice Peacemaker—or anyone else. He was like a wary, half-wild cat who'd ventured into a warm farm kitchen and needed first to peer into every crack and corner. The partly open door to the body of the meetinghouse seemed especially to draw him.

Mr. Lawson turned to Rob and murmured, "Well, he is here now. Proceed with your question, pray."

"Yes, sir," said Rob. "Mr. Cranshaw," he began, in a louder voice.

The old man turned, looking startled. "Aye?"

"Do you recognize this youth?"

Eben glanced at Peacemaker. "Aye. 'Tis the shade of Young-John Morton," he said, resuming his prowling.

"There!" screeched Peacemaker. "I told you! He is a madman! He seeth nothing but ghosts and the fires of the world's end! What can *he*—?"

"Silence!" Mr. Lawson shouted. "*I* will continue the questioning now."

He walked up to Eben and tapped his shoulder.

"Mr. Cranshaw, did you see this—er—shade on Thursday afternoon?"

"Aye. On Thursday afternoon. When the minister be lecturing." Eben glanced at Peacemaker. "I see 'un everywhere, these days."

Still quietly, Mr. Lawson continued, "And what was he doing on Thursday afternoon, pray?"

"He come slinking up like the ghost he is," said Eben. "And he placeth the creature's corse under the tree. The corse with the message from God enstamped upon it. To say the end of the world be nigh."

"You lie, you old fool, you lie!" Peacemaker was jumping up and down. "How *could* you see, fool? You had your back to the street and your ear pressed to . . . the wall at . . . the side. . . ."

His voice had faltered and faded as they all stared at him. All except Eben, who was now gazing into the larger room where he'd once listened to sermons and prayed with his wife and all the rest of the community.

But Mr. Lawson was now addressing Peacemaker. "So riddle me this, then, *rascal.* How come you know what Mr. Cranshaw was doing *outside,* when you were *inside,* listening to the lecture?"

Peacemaker's mouth opened, then shut, then opened and shut again.

"He be a shade, and shades can see through walls," said Eben in a preoccupied voice, still gazing into the main part of the meetinghouse.

Suddenly Hester felt a huge surge of hope. She could see the effect that that last casual remark of Eben's had had on the two men. They might just have been prepared to believe that the devil could have taken possession of the cat's body. But they knew for a fact that Peacemaker was not a ghost with the power to see through timber!

As for Peacemaker, his face was a picture of utter bafflement. For an instant he'd looked as if he might even have snatched at the crazy excuse the old man had offered for him. But then he must have realized that it was of no help to his cause whatsoever.

"Well?" said Mr. Phipps. "Hast thou lost thy tongue?"

"I—" Peacemaker was squirming. "I—he lies! I—I—"

"Go!" thundered Mr. Lawson. "Go now, at once, and

bring your father! I intend to put you on your oath, and we shall require him—both as your parent and as town marshal—to witness your answers when I repeat my questions!"

"Y-yes, sir," whispered Peacemaker.

As he stumbled out, he himself seemed to be seeing a vision of the end of the world. And judging from his face, thought Hester, it could hardly have been a whit less terrifying than old Eben's inferno!

15
The Search

But after they'd waited thirty minutes, Hester and Rob were sent across to find out the cause of the delay.

And no, Peacemaker had not even spoken to his father. All he'd done, according to Mistress Cleary, was stuff his sack with sugar buns and venison pie before hurrying off. And then—after Mr. Lawson had explained to Ezra Cleary just why his presence had been required and they'd made another search in and around the tavern—they realized what had happened.

"The dog!" roared Mr. Cleary. "He must a lit out for the forest! He hath taken the old wheel-lock pistol from the wall—with powder and shot, no doubt!"

"Oh, Lord!" cried Mistress Cleary. "I hope he don't think to shoot hisself, him being so sinfully accused an' all!"

"Not he!" growled her husband. "But I'll tell you this, woman! He'll wish he *had*, when I get a hold of him—bringing this disgrace on us!"

When Peacemaker hadn't shown up by nightfall, Mr. Cleary softened a little. "He'll be back when he's hungry!" he muttered.

Meanwhile, Hester's own concern had been growing. "I can't help thinking about that pistol," she said. "Who is he designing to use it on? Himself—as his mother seems to think?"

"Peacemaker Cleary? Never!" said Rob.

"On *us,* then?"

"Ha! Let him but try!"

"Or Mr. Cranshaw?"

"Nonsense!" jeered Rob. "The fool will be hoping to kill game with it when his food runs out. Or merely to light fires with its flash."

They were discussing this in the woodshed. Hester gazed down at her record book. She hadn't meant it to end like this.

"But what if something happens to him?" she said.

Rob looked completely unconcerned. "He is a cheat and a liar and a coward," he said. "He is less than the dirt."

"But he can't just be allowed to *die!*" she said.

Rob shrugged. "Why not? He deserves to die!"

"Because—because that wouldn't be *just!*" she said. "If he hadn't run away, he would have been fittingly punished. But not by *hanging.*"

"Ha! *Goody Willson* would have been hung if he had continued in his lies! And so would other innocents."

She frowned. "Yes," she said. "But we have put a stop to that. The whole town knows now that it was all a lie."

"And he tried to kill the cat," said Rob, unmoved.

"He did not then!" said Hester.

"No?"

"No. You said yourself. It was an accident. The fallen

chimney stone. In the picture you described, first to me, then to Mistress Brown and Nell."

Rob smiled grimly. "That was only my bright picture," he said.

She stared at him. "Your *bright* picture?"

"Yes," he said. "I sometimes see two. One bright, one dark. I told you only the bright one, because I know how it pains you to hear of—of what you call cruelty. What I, too, now call cruelty."

She thought again of the dragonfly and bit on her lower lip.

"So . . . what was your dark picture?"

"I saw him using that stone to club the cat with. I saw him pick it up and turn to the tethered cat and—"

"Stop! You said it *fell* on the cat because of the thunderclap."

"In my bright picture, yes," he said. "But in my dark picture it was lying there already. Having fallen some days or weeks ago in some other storm."

She gave her hair a scornful toss. "Well, I don't believe your dark picture then! The bright one is much more likely. With the prospect of earning a shilling or two with the living cat, Peacemaker Cleary wasn't going to risk killing it."

Rob was silent for a few moments. Then: "In his lying confession, he himself talked of throwing rocks at it."

"Those *were* just lies," said Hester. "And anyway, the creature is now on the mend, thanks to your ministrations. She doesn't even have a broken leg, after all—as you proclaimed only this afternoon. And tomorrow Goody Willson will be well enough for them to be restored one to the other."

Rob's expression set stonily again. "But none of that is thanks to Peacemaker Cleary. He tried to have Goody Willson hung."

She sighed. "But he will be punished for what he did! Appropriately. In a civilized way!"

He grunted. "I tell you, I am not interested in what happens to such dirt. Anyway, he'll come crawling back soon enough when he feels the first hunger pangs. Even as his father said."

But, hungry or not, Peacemaker did not return that day.

The next morning, when they went down onto the main street to glean what news there was, they were confronted with a general air of consternation.

No, the boy had not returned.

Aye, search parties had been dispatched. Ever since dawn.

And although it was bright enough, the air had that chill in it from the north that spoke of a heavy snowfall to come before long. Everyone was talking about it— some of them looking at Rob and Hester with a glimmer of accusation in their eyes.

So *Hester* fancied, anyway.

"He could be dead already," she whispered.

She was feeling really low and miserable. The idea that she and Rob might have driven Peacemaker to his death had given her a very restless night.

All Rob did was shrug.

"He might have been devoured by wolves!" she persisted.

"He might," he said.

"Or bit by a rattlesnake!"

He smiled a thin smile. "Too early. They will still be sleeping."

She began to feel angry. "Or—or killed by Indians!" she said.

His eyes lit up. "That depends."

"Depends on what?"

"Whether it be a hunting party he blunders into, or a war party."

"What difference will *that* make?"

"A hunting party will have no interest in such. So long as he doesn't try to fight them. Which—unless it be a hunting party of kittens—he won't dare to do."

"And a war party?"

This time he grinned. "Ah, *well . . .*," he said.

Hester's spirits sank even further. "Most likely he could die from the cold," she said hurriedly, trying to strike a less lurid note. "If there *is* a blizzard."

"He can light a fire," Rob murmured.

"If he has tumbled into a ravine and broke his leg—" she began. Then, seeing his still-unmoved expression, she gave the frozen mud a stamp. "Oh, you are hopeless!"

But as the search parties came drifting back, shaking their heads, Rob began to pick up interest. "They have no method!" he muttered. "They have no patience! They should not be returning so soon!"

"But one of them was saying they *did* find signs of his having slept at the Morton place. With fir branches for his bed and warm ashes in the hearth."

"Huh! I could a pictured that without setting foot out

of town," said Rob. "Didn't Eben tell us how he often saw the shade of Young-John Morton visit the ruins? That was one of *Peacemaker Cleary's* regular haunts."

"Well," Hester began thoughtfully, "I suppose—"

"But what happened after they found the signs?" said Rob. "Who tried to pick up the trail from thence? Nothing and no one!"

At last, Hester saw her chance. "Well, they are not trained trackers like you," she said quietly. "Though I don't suppose even you could have done any better."

He swung on her. "Oh, no?"

"No," she said. "He could have gone off in any direction. And with the frost making the ground hard, he will have made no footprints in the soft earth or—"

"What? Put on your stouter shoes, Hester Bidgood! Fore fit thyself for tracking in the forest, and I will show you! Ground too hard!"

Soon afterward, they were both standing in the withered grass at the far side of the Morton ruins. Hester had not only put on her stouter shoes but also an extra pair of thick woolen stockings, and had armed herself with a sturdy ash-plant staff. Rob himself had thrown the tartan blanket over his shoulders. Otherwise he was wearing his everyday leggings and moccasins, together with his hunting knife and medicine bag. She hoped he'd brought something to tend to any injuries their quarry might have.

If they ever found him!

It seemed very unlikely at first. The grass had already been trampled by themselves, on Saturday, and now there were signs of many more investigators.

"The *search* party!" Rob kept muttering, sounding very sarcastic as he prowled around, peering.

Then, even as they began slowly to circle the area beyond the grass, they heard voices. It was another search party, coming down through the trees.

"'Tis no use looking up there," one of the men said, jerking his thumb back to where the first slopes of Morton's Mountain began to rise.

"No signs at all?" said Rob.

"Ne'er a one."

Rob and Hester knew the men, of course.

"Farmers!" murmured Rob as the party tramped off down toward the village. "What would they know if they *did* see a sign?"

"As much as we do now," said Hester gloomily.

"Even so," said Rob, "*I* picture him headed up there. . . . Come, do not loiter."

At first it was like their search in the forest on Friday. But this time the going was harder; the undergrowth, thicker; and what animal tracks there were, more obscure. Hester kept catching her skirts on thorns, even though she'd hitched them almost to her knees. She found herself very glad of the staff, which she used to help hack a path through the brush—but it wasn't long before Rob said, "Thou'rt making too much noise."

"What does it matter?" she said. "We're not tracking down an animal, hoping to take it unawares and kill it."

He grunted but didn't argue further. "Very well," he said. "But see you keep behind me."

He himself proceeded in his usual silence, carefully picking his way, pausing, peering around. Only once did he turn and break that silence. He was grinning. "By the way, there may be other ears than Peacemaker's to hear thy thrashings about."

"I told you already," she retorted. "We are not tracking animals."

"I do not mean animals," he said. "How be if those Indians you spoke of so fearfully are somewhere about?"

Suddenly she felt her heart bumping. "I—well—you—you would be able to speak with them in their own tongue and tell them we mean them no harm. . . . Wouldn't you?"

At this, despite all his earlier cautions, he laughed aloud. "Think you that all Indians are friendly toward other Indians? Why, if the language I used proved to be that of an enemy tribe, our scalps would be hanging from their belts sooner than you could say 'knife!' "

Hester kept the noise of her thrashing down to the merest whisper after that.

Then, on a patch of moss where a powdering of recent snow had settled, Rob found what he'd been looking for. A single footprint, showing a lighter impression at the outer edge of the heel.

"Yes," he said. "I had pictured aright. He is heading up toward the top of Morton's Mountain." He looked at the footprint again. "And it was not much more than an hour ago that he left this sign."

16
The Catamount

It was well past noon before they finally tracked him down, three-quarters of the way up Morton's Mountain. Sometimes it had seemed as if they were not going uphill at all, when they went plunging down sudden hollows to the banks of streams before climbing again.

In one such dell, Rob lost the track for a while. The undergrowth was dense with laurel bushes and the creeping roots and stems of what they knew as wintergreen, with slippery, leathery leaves. This made the going treacherous, on slopes as steep as this. They had reached the bottom, near a fast-flowing creek, and Rob was at the water's edge, looking for any signs of Peacemaker's trail, when Hester herself spotted the crucial sign.

"Look!" she said. "Isn't that a sack up there?" She was pointing to an oak tree, about twenty paces away.

Rob approached it cautiously. The sack had been caught on the jagged stump of a torn-off branch, about eight feet from the ground.

"It—it does look like Peacemaker's herb sack," said Hester. "Doesn't it?"

Rob jumped up, grabbing it. "Yes," he murmured. "It is. . . ."

He stood back, looking up at the tree. There were no leaves, but it was a mature tree, and the masses of branches and twigs made it difficult to see to the top.

"Do you think he is up there?" Hester asked.

Rob laughed softly. "Not Peacemaker . . . no. But"— he was stooping to examine some fresh scars on the trunk—"the *bear* probably is."

"Bear?" Hester gasped.

"Aye. These be her claw marks. Also those, higher up. See?"

While Hester was staring up, Rob calmly turned and looked around.

"And yes," he murmured. "Yon log by the creek. That is where he would have chosen to sit. Where he would be just about to enjoy what was left of his buns, when the bear caught a whiff of the sugar or honey or whatever Mistress Cleary puts inside them."

"But " Hester glanced back at the tree. "Peace-maker? Where is—?"

"'Tis all right. The bear will not have dragged *him* up. They don't eat flesh. Not when there are sweetmeats to be had." Rob gazed across the creek and up the opposite slope. "Peacemaker will have fled as fast as his legs could carry him."

He turned back to the log. "There, see," he said, pointing to some grayish white dust spilled partly on the log itself and partly on the ground. "Powder. Peacemaker will have had the fright of his life when he saw Mistress Bear. I see him trying to load that foolish pistol, then realizing there would not be time, thrusting it in his belt, and fleeing up yonder. That is my picture."

"But where?" said Hester.

"Oh, not far," said Rob. "Only to find some secure hiding place. Some place he could hope to defend with a pistol. Where he would have time to load it before the bear came seeking him. There is a bluff at the top, see. And where there's a bluff, there usually be clefts and caverns."

Hester stared up at the reddish gold cliff showing through the trees. She was wondering how long it would take *them* to reach it.

"What if the bear follows us?"

"I hear no signs of her movements. Probably she is still too sleepy."

"But if she *does*? *We* have no pistol! Where are you going?"

Rob was already back beside the oak tree, examining a fallen branch. Then, swiftly, methodically, he began trimming it with his knife. Within a couple of minutes he came back to her with a six-foot lance, sharply forked at the end.

"This would be all we'd need," he said. "This and to keep quite calm and still and resolute."

His manner reassured her more than the pike itself. But not entirely.

"You were saying you thought Peacemaker was up there."

"That is my picture. Let us see if it be accurate."

It began to seem likely. Halfway up the slope they

found Peacemaker's hat, caught in a laurel bush, and at the top, where the bluff rose sheer above them, there was indeed a cavern.

Hester wondered if it was the one from which Eben hoped to watch the end of the century and of the world. Its entrance opened out three or four feet above a rocky ledge. The ledge itself was approached by a steep narrow path on one side and a longer, wider path on the other. The steep path was nearer and that was the one they took, Rob in the lead.

When he was just below the entrance, Rob stopped and bent down. The ledge was at its widest here, and what he'd seen seemed to interest him greatly. He motioned her to keep back while he studied a cluster of paw marks—some quite large, some smaller. They seemed to have been made when the ground was softer, and were now frozen in. Unfortunately, any powdery snow that had fallen up here lately had been blown away, so there was no way of telling if Peacemaker Cleary himself had passed over that surface. Not in Hester's eyes, anyway.

Rob, however, was still engrossed in the animal prints. "A catamount's" he murmured. "A catamount with one—yes—just one kitten. Born late in the season, probably. She must be getting old. But old or not, I wouldn't wish to be in Peacemaker's shoon if—"

"*Avoid!*"

Hester gave a little scream, but Rob was smiling as he looked up at the mouth of the cave, where Peacemaker was now crouching, brandishing his pistol. "Avoid or I shoot!"

He looked terrible. His face was whiter than ever. His

eyes were bulging. His hair hung matted over his ears and shoulders. There was a long tear in one of his sleeves, and the strings of his breeches were straggling loose.

"We have come to take you back," Hester said, not caring for the way the muzzle of the pistol kept wavering in her direction, but speaking up as stoutly as she could.

"Avoid, I say! Keep back!"

"Your mother is worried sick about you," said Hester.

"*That* old cow!" Peacemaker snarled.

Hester was genuinely shocked. "How could you speak like that of your own mother!"

"At least he didn't call her an old squaw," said Rob.

"'Tis my father I'm worried about!" growled the fugitive, this time waving the muzzle toward Rob. "He will skin me alive, I know he will, and I *won't* be took back!"

"But your father is speaking much more leniently this morning," said Hester. "He declares that so long as you come back alive, he will be well content."

"He be a liar!" said Peacemaker. "He be the lyingest person I know, save you two. He will flog me something terrible." His voice took on a whining note. "And the more he flogs me, the more furious do he wax. I know *him*. . . . Avoid! Or I will shoot!"

Rob shrugged. "Save thy powder and shot, if there be any left. You are like to need it before long."

Peacemaker twitched. "Eh? Why? What for?"

"The bear, for one—" Rob began.

"Well . . ." Peacemaker's leer began to spread. "Well, as to *that*, 'twill attack you out there first. And when it has ate you both, 'twill be too sleepy to bother with *me*."

"Ah, but the catamount will not be too sleepy," said Rob.

"Eh? *What* catamount?"

"The one that lives in there with her kitten."

Peacemaker took a quick backward glance. "Thou liest!" he said. "There be neither cat nor kit in here!"

"No. She is out hunting. But when she returns to her kitten—"

"Liar! I would a seen the kitten!"

"If you had eyes or ears, you would," said Rob. "Do you not know the ways of a wild creature? She will have hid it in a cranny and told it to lie still—still as death—if some intruder enters. Go see for yourself."

The crafty leer slowly returned. "What? And turn my back on *you* two treachers? Avoid!"

"Oh, well," said Rob, "let us leave the fool, Hester. Even without the pistol, he is so brave and fearless with cats and their young. Why, he should be able to fight off the raging mother with rocks. Aye, and brand her, also." He looked up at the now-gaping Peacemaker. "Hast thou got the *T* iron with you? And tinder to kindle the fire?"

"No—I—I don't know what you mean. I—"

"No? Well, then, we will go back and fetch them for you. Let us hope we return before the catamount. Come, Hester, we—"

Hester's heart missed a beat as Rob's banter was interrupted by the most bloodcurdling sound she had ever heard—a high scream that tapered off into a shrill, piercing, whistling noise.

"Wha-what was *that*?" gasped Peacemaker.

"Keep out of sight if you value your miserable life!" said Rob. "'Tis she!"

Hester stared with horror down the longer path leading to the rocks at the edge of the forest below. Colored like the rocks herself, the half-crouching creature had just emerged from the trees and was now staring up at them, ears flattened, its long, black-tipped tail slowly swishing.

17
The Coward

"She is in some doubt," murmured Rob. "She is not sure whether we have found her kitten or not."

"Is—is it—?" came the hoarse whisper from above.

"Keep quiet, fool!" said Rob softly.

Then suddenly, to Hester's amazement, he smiled. It was that thin, cruel smile she so hated.

"If we left now," he said, "the way we came, she would be content."

"But what of Peacemaker?"

"He did great evil to a cat," Rob said. "'Tis only just that a cat do great evil to him."

"That is not justice!" she protested.

"It is the justice of the wild."

"It is not the justice of *humans*!"

"The justice of *humans*!" he jeered. "They who'd hang an old woman because she talks to a bird? What—?"

"Look out!" gasped Hester.

The catamount had begun to inch forward, its ears still flattened.

Rob stepped a pace toward it. Then he stood with the lance in front of him, the fork's prongs about three feet from the ground.

Over his shoulder, he said, "Go now. Down the other path. Sideways, taking care not to show her your back."

Hester was trembling. "I will do no such thing! Not unless Peacemaker goes with us!"

"Aye!" came a hoarse plea. "She—she speaks wisely! She knows 'tis only I who have a pistol!"

"Your pistol will not be worth a sugar bun if this cat gets past me," said Rob, still keeping his eyes on the creature. "Now listen, fool. Your only chance is to flush out that kit and let it run to its mother. Then, seeing it be safe, she will—"

The catamount had moved forward another few inches. Rob remained still as a post.

"—she will have no interest in such as thee."

"Yes, hurry, Peacemaker!" said Hester.

"I—I—"

"*Hurry!*"

He darted out of sight.

Then: "Oh!" she heard him cry.

"Do you see it?" said Hester.

"Oh, but it be *large!*" came the wail. "It be bigger than Goody Pierce's bad, fat, old red cat! And—ow!—it hisseth at me!"

Over his shoulder, Rob said, "Throw him your stick, Hester. Tell him to drive it out with that if he's afraid of a few scratches. But hurry! She will soon be within springing distance!"

Even as he was speaking, Hester had clambered into

the cavern herself. It was dim in there, but light enough to see Peacemaker Cleary sitting on a boulder, blubbering, shaking with fright.

"Where—?" she began.

He was pointing abjectly into a corner. Then she saw it. It *was* big. And it was spitting furiously.

But she kept a tight grip on the staff and gently but firmly steered the creature forward. Suddenly there came another chilling scream from outside. Her heart seemed to stop. Was the catamount even now clawing at Rob's face?

But the kitten had heard it, too, and with a squeal of its own, it shot forward over Peacemaker's outstretched legs and into the daylight. For a split second, Hester found herself marveling at the creature's speckled body. She hadn't known that catamount kittens were marked like that.

"Come on! Quickly!"

Rob's head and shoulders appeared at the entrance. He reached in and helped her down. She was vastly relieved to see the mother cat back at the bottom of the path again. She was crouching over her hulking, great kitten, growling, sniffing, and licking it. Hester shuddered at the sight of the big cat's tongue and teeth, crimson and white, which seconds earlier might have been tearing and savoring Rob's flesh.

"Wait for me!" cried Peacemaker as Rob began to steer Hester away.

"Take thy time, fool!" Rob called back. "The mother is too busy to trouble herself over *you.*"

"But she will be seeking revenge!"

"Revenge for what?" said Rob. "You did no harm to *this* young creature."

"But—she is looking at us!" said Peacemaker, still cowering at the mouth of the cave.

And indeed so she was, but only in a cautiously watchful way as the kitten clung to the ruff of fur at her neck.

Rob grinned. "Aye, so she is!" he said. "She hath her eye on thee, Peacemaker Cleary! Jump for your life and join us before it be too late!"

And jump Peacemaker Cleary did, even forgetting the pistol in his panicky eagerness to put them and their sticks between himself and the catamount.

Only when they were plunging through the laurels did he remember it. "My pistol!" he cried. "I left it behind!"

"Then go back for it," said Rob. "But don't expect us to wait. The sky is growing uncommon leaden. And if the blizzard don't catch up with us, the bear might!"

Peacemaker didn't mention the pistol again, all the way back.

As they came within sight of the village and the first fast, fat snowflakes began to swirl around them, Hester heard a low, hissing, gurgling noise and turned. To her surprise, she saw that Rob was shaking with half-suppressed laughter.

"What is so amusing?" she said.

He jerked his head back at the stumbling figure trying to keep up with them. "Him," said Rob.

"What about him?"

"I was just thinking of the way he looked when he came flying out of the cavern. With his arms flailing up and his legs all awry." Rob wiped away snowflakes that were gathering on his cheeks, along with tears of pure childish merriment.

"It does not seem so funny to *me*," she said.

"No, but—for an instant—with his arms and legs just so—he formed a perfect letter *K*."

"Hey! Wait for me!" bleated Peacemaker.

"Don't worry! We're safe now," Hester called back contemptuously. She turned to Rob again. "What is so funny about Peacemaker Cleary making the letter *K*?"

"Why, don't you see?" he said, beginning to laugh again. "'Twas so fitting! *K* for *coward*!"

She closed her eyes against a sudden flurry of flakes.

"The sooner we resume your schooling, the better," she said dryly.

But now she was feeling glad—really glad. His mind seemed still to be set on more important things than hunting, after all.

Which left her free to enjoy, without any further disturbing shadows, the scoring of her first victory as Hester Bidgood, Investigatrix of Evill Deedes.